The Tulip Factory

The Tulip Factory

KACIE DAVIS IDOL

INKSHARES

Copyright © 2016 Kacie Davis Idol

Published by Inkshares, Inc., San Francisco, California
www.inkshares.com

Edited and designed by Girl Friday Productions
www.girlfridayproductions.com
Cover design by Anna Curtis

Cover images © dpproductions/iStockphoto;
© RiverNorthPhotography/iStockphoto; © mcswin/iStockphoto

ISBN: 9781941758779
e-ISBN: 9781941758786
Library of Congress Control Number: 2015951538

First edition

Printed in the United States of America

This book is dedicated to my sweet Finnley.
If happiness does not find you, seek it.

PROLOGUE

CORINNE

When I was little, I was the flower girl in my aunt's wedding. She was your true eighties rocker chick, and even in 1990, she was still clinging to her preferred decade, shoulder pads and all. The late-spring wedding was full of blue dresses, yellow corsages, and really big hair.

I can remember it like it was yesterday; we were sitting in the elders' room of my family's church before the ceremony. The scent of hair spray and old hymnals permeated the air. Back then my hair was much blonder and way curlier than it is now, and my mom had neatly pulled the front back with an oversize yellow bow. I sat on the floor in the corner of the room, twirling my empty flower girl basket in circles. It was painted white and had a yellow ribbon threaded through the handle to complement the wedding theme.

The florist had just arrived with a cardboard box full of carefully arranged white roses, also tied with yellow ribbons. She began passing out the bouquets to the bridal party, starting with the bride. One by one, the overzealous group of women in their puffy-sleeved dresses and stiff bangs eagerly took their budding bundles. I waited patiently with my empty basket for my white rose petals to sprinkle down the aisle.

My parents had been talking me up for weeks, so I was excited for my big debut. I had practiced multiple times during the wedding rehearsal, and I knew exactly when to walk and where to stand. I was a quiet child. I did what I was told without causing a scene, and I didn't like getting into trouble. Once all the bouquets had been handed out, the giddy bridal party beamed proudly and got into position, ready to make their way down the aisle. That's when my mom came in to check on everyone and to join the procession as the matron of honor. Noticing my bare basket, she hurried over and squatted down beside me, getting on my level.

"Sweetie, where are your rose petals?" she asked.

I had never gotten my rose petals. The florist had completely forgotten them. My aunt began freaking out, the florist started to panic, and the bridesmaids kept teasing their hair, pretending to be worried at the same time. Just then, my dad came busting through the door like a superhero. (Maybe he didn't "bust" through the door, but that's how it plays out in my memory.) He came straight over to me, and my mom told him about the latest wedding debacle. She was shaking her head and trying to calm my aunt by offering to tear some petals off of her own bouquet for me to throw. Apparently that wasn't an option. That's when my dad spoke up. He announced that he had an idea, kissed my mom on the cheek, and left the room in a hurry.

My aunt paced the floor and stared at the clock. It was a small room, and it was starting to feel smaller by the second. My stomach rumbled from hunger, and the hair spray fumes were making me dizzy. Just as I thought I was going to have to eat the sugar cubes next to the coffeemaker, my dad came running through the door. His cheeks were flushed and he was out of breath. Before my mom could even ask where he had been for the last ten minutes, he made a beeline for me, holding something wrapped in brown paper.

He unwrapped the thin package and pulled out a handful of fresh yellow tulips. He eased himself down to the floor by my side and smiled. My aunt peered over his shoulder and commented on how the flowers didn't look like roses. He immediately shushed her. Not only were they not roses, but they were certainly not white. He started pulling the petals off and dropping them into my basket, then handed me the other tulips and told me to do the same. My dad had saved the day and also my shining moment as a flower girl. I'll never forget what he said to me next.

"This is your moment, baby girl. If the world is all white roses, then you're a field of tulips."

CHAPTER 1

THE MORNING AFTER

The sunlight spilled into the bedroom through the faded gold curtains and onto the pillow, illuminating Corinne's wavy blonde hair. The young woman lay nestled in her queen-size bed, entangled in a white duvet fit for a king, still wearing her clothes from the evening before. Most mornings, she'd have been up and out on a nearby running trail for half an hour by now, and she would be showered, dolled up, and ready for the day before the sun had even made its way over the North Carolina coast. Most mornings, she'd be composed and cheery as she greeted the locals at her favorite coffeehouse just two blocks away from where she lived. And she certainly would not be hungover as hell. But today was proving to be unlike most mornings. She turned on her side, and before she could use her forearm as a shield, a beam of sunlight stabbed her directly in the eyes. Slowly, she began to reopen them and noticed the room was a little blurry. So was her mind.

Wait, this is my room, right? she thought, but before panic could set in, she noticed Charlie lying at the foot of her bed, possibly judging her with his big brown eyes. Everything came into focus as she used her elbows to prop herself up. Charlie had been Corinne's right-hand man for going on nine years now. He had dark-brown fur, four legs, and a tail. His stout physique gave him a bearlike appearance; he was definitely the kind of dog you didn't approach or mess with unless you knew him. He lifted his head and started to wag his tail at the sight of Corinne sitting up, then began whining, informing her that it was past time for breakfast. The thought of food made her stomach turn. Charlie hadn't gotten completely wasted last night, so he was ready for the day, while she was ready for an aspirin. It felt like the word "irresponsible" should be stamped on her forehead. Squinting, her eyes barely open, and one hand on her nightstand, she rolled to her right, holding on for support. Her weight caused the table to shift and a slender blue vase of flourishing white tulips to teeter for a second before settling back down. *Crisis averted,* she thought as her feet touched the cold hardwood floor.

She felt old. Not "retire to the Florida Keys" kind of old but maybe too old to be staying out drinking all night long. She had been able to do that in her early twenties, but she was officially an adult now, twenty-eight years old, self-sufficient, with a good job. Well, that last part was debatable; nonetheless, it was a job. Her writing career hadn't exactly taken off like she had hoped it would, so after college, and more years of waiting tables than expected, she'd taken a position through a temp agency as a receptionist at a dental office. That was all it was supposed to be: temporary—a stepping-stone. But that's how things go; stepping-stones become familiar and comfortable, and before she knew it, she had lost sight of her dreams. Either way, dream or reality, today she was faced with life; she had responsibilities, bills, and people and a pet counting on her, regardless of her hangover.

Imagining the feel of the cool wooden floor against her face, she gingerly eased her way down the side of her bed, her temples throbbing. She curled up into the fetal position and laid her burning cheek on the smooth planks. It was instant relief for her pounding head, even though she was now face-to-face with the layer of dust that covered her floor. The sun highlighted the dust particles, causing the warped wood to sparkle. It was actually kind of pretty, but it also reminded her of the housework that would most certainly be neglected today.

However, not everything or *everyone* could be put on the back burner. Charlie stood over her, licking her face in an effort to get her back on her feet. Careful not to use the nightstand for leverage this time, she used the bedsheets to pull herself up and then let out a deep breath as if strained from the effort of standing. Sluggishly shuffling her feet, she made her way to the kitchen with Charlie on her heels. Since his breakfast was coming later than usual, she scooped him an extra-large helping of dry dog food. He dove in headfirst before she could even finish pouring it into his bright-blue bowl. His eagerness reminded her of her need for caffeine.

Corinne had no qualms about living the single life. Honestly, she had grown accustomed to it, especially since most of her friends were married. She shopped alone and jogged alone; she had perfected the art of cooking for one and brewing just enough for a single cup of coffee. Today, however, she felt that a full pot would be necessary. As the coffee began to drip slowly, she sat down at the small bistro-style table and rested her head heavily in the palm of her hand.

She struggled to remember the events of the night before. A few years ago, partying like that would've been a typical Saturday night for her, but those kinds of outings were few and far between now, verging on the cusp of never. Weddings, however, were always an exception. *Weddings are my kryptonite,* she thought to herself with a wry smile. The sun beamed through the thinning leaves on the trees, causing her to squint. It was truly a beautiful Sunday morning, and her head filled with images of foamy drinks spilling onto her dress and how she'd stumbled while getting out of a cab. Then, suddenly, it hit her.

"I called him!" Corinne shrieked out loud. "Seriously? Why, why, why?" In an effort to make sense of her audacious behavior, she began going over their timeline in her head, replaying and obsessing over her last few encounters with James.

"Okay," she started, while motioning to an imaginary chart, "he called me on my twenty-fifth birthday, which was like a month after we decided to call it quits, and then I called *him* the night of Ava's wedding, and, yes, I happened to be intoxicated that night as well. That wasn't even six months after the breakup, so naturally I would have had a weak moment. My judgment was cloudy, and someone probably should've stopped me."

And someone *had* tried to stop her. She recalled the beautiful, chilly spring evening in 2012, two years ago, when her little sister, Ava, had gotten married. Corinne had been newly single and, most importantly, the maid of honor. Her date for that evening was a bottle of moderately priced champagne. (Contrary to popular belief, the more expensive price had not helped with the hangover the next morning. Cheap champagne, expensive champagne—either way you're doomed after the fifth glass.) Ava had known a lot about James, mostly from long-winded stories Corinne would share with her over the phone, since they didn't live in the same town. Corinne had spent as many hours obsessing over him during their relationship as she did dwelling on him after it ended. On the night of the wedding, as Ava was being pulled into the limo by her groom, she had pleaded with a very intoxicated Corinne not to call or text him. Thinking back on it now, Corinne shook her head, embarrassed all over again at the memory.

Redirecting her attention back to the timeline, she recalled the few times she had seen him in passing. Not long after their breakup, these encounters were often at their favorite coffee shop, which he had eventually stopped frequenting. Things really started to change, though, when they stopped seeing each other as much. At first, the brushes had been genuine and pleasant, but they'd soon turned awkward, with uncomfortable lulls in the already watered-down conversations. The sincerity of their brief encounters eventually disappeared, and small talk and a casual "hello" were all that was left.

Pressing on her forehead, Corinne strained to remember the last time she had seen James. "Oh yeah," she announced. Charlie cocked his head to the side. "We ran into each other at The Walkmen concert . . . last summer? Wow, more than a year ago." She was surprised by this realization. Time had definitely gotten away from her. And now, after almost a year, the "drunk dial" had reared its ugly head again. Unable to remember what she had said or if he had even answered her call, Corinne felt her headache also rear its ugly head.

The entire kitchen was rich with the scent of hazelnut coffee, her favorite. She walked over to the cupboard where she kept her coffee mugs. Actually, the only cups she owned were coffee mugs and a few sets of red wineglasses; she drank almost everything out of her mugs. She pulled out an over-size cream-colored ceramic one with thick red stripes and a pale-pink floral print dotting the entire rim. She filled the mug with coffee, adding only cream. Taking a quick glance out of her kitchen window, she saw a soft shower of orange and yellow leaves finally making their way from the trees down to the earth. It seemed like autumn had arrived overnight, which made her very happy, since fall was without a doubt her favorite season. She relaxed a little and began to feel much lighter about everything.

"I'm sure he didn't even answer his phone," she told Charlie. Feeling more confident, she reassured herself out loud again. "Of course he didn't answer the phone. It was the middle of the night, and he was probably asleep or busy doing something else . . . something more interesting than answering phone calls from drunken ex-girlfriends. Hopefully he assumes it was a pocket dial." Charlie seemed bored by her rambling and laid his head back down on the floor that was now all warmed up from the sunshine. Corinne thought back to a few years before.

Remembering the time they spent together as a couple, she was immediately flooded with the most amazing memories; the good ones were always the longest lasting. The thoughts sent an instant zing to her heart, and she quickly had to remind herself of the end: the jealousy and late nights that led to irrational words and actions. She remembered the horrible feeling of almost losing herself as he became her primary focus. And who could forget the embarrassing display of his record collection scattered across the front yard . . .

Corinne shrugged her tense shoulders and rolled her neck around to rid her mind of these thoughts and then took a long sip of her coffee. Staring at a short cylindrical vase with a small cluster of orange tulips peeking over the rim, she found herself thinking back to the beginning of everything, and that early morning in her favorite coffee shop during the winter of 2009.

CHAPTER 2

AT FIRST SIGHT

CORINNE

It was the end of a relatively uneventful 2009, the new year just weeks away. The dull nature of it wasn't necessarily a bad thing; it's just where I was in my life at that time. I had graduated from the University of North Carolina at Wilmington the previous year in 2008 and spent that whole summer going out with friends and attempting to surf. Early the following fall, I had finally gotten a job waiting tables at a ritzy, upscale joint near Wrightsville Beach. We opened only in the evening hours for dinner, so I found my days pretty free, but I didn't mind it one bit. Having spent the last four years writing papers, constructing presentations, and, my all-time favorite, learning "critical thinking," some free time felt like a well-deserved break. And I really had no idea what I wanted to do with the bachelor's degree in communications I'd earned, so I decided to take the server position to fill the gap. Little did I know that "gap" would last for roughly four years. Despite my big plans during college for what I'd do postgraduation, I was totally content, and my parents weren't pressuring me to find a different job as long as I wasn't hitting them up for money.

My parents were awesome. They had always been super supportive of most of my decisions, and they also knew me well enough to know I'm not the self-destructive type. It's not in my nature. Growing up, I was a pretty focused kid; I did well in school, never got into any real trouble, and was somewhat athletic—"athletic" meaning I had energy and stamina, but I lacked the competitive gene, so I never went anywhere with sports. Another thing that let my parents sleep better at night was that I never really went boy crazy like most of my friends did after the age of thirteen. I was single for much of my time at UNCW, with two exceptions, the first being Christopher. We met our freshman year, living in the same dorm—thank God for coed, right? He was a tall and tan soccer player with blue eyes and surfer hair. He was my first for a lot of things, and there were many times during our off-and-on two-year relationship that I truly thought it could be love, and a few times I even convinced myself that it was. But young love is often reckless and unpredictable, and in the end it just wasn't meant to be, so we amicably split during our sophomore year. I came out the other side unscathed and with a lifelong friend.

The other "relationship," if you can call it that, was a three-month fling with a guy from work who will remain nameless. It was the summer before my junior year, and I had just started my first waitressing job so I could support myself and stay in Wilmington for the summer instead of going back home. I hadn't been working at the restaurant long when he made his move. He seemed so different from the boys I was used to, probably because he wasn't a *boy* at all! It caught me off guard for sure; he was nine years older than me with a thousand lines I'd never heard before, not to mention his own house. I was so naïve about the whole thing. It took me longer than it should have, but eventually I discovered what he was really all about. It wasn't all bad; I look back at it like growing pains, and plus, I learned a lot about life and myself through that experience. I finally wised up and called it quits in September 2006. He caused a scene. It was a bit awkward working together for a while after that, but luckily a blue-eyed twenty-year-old student was hired part-time as a hostess in early December, and, just like that, I was off the hook.

Now, a few years later, I had a little money in the bank and a low-maintenance lifestyle, and I knew almost nothing about loss and even less about love. Life was easy. But I soon learned, when life is letting you enjoy the view, it's really just giving you a chance to catch your breath.

The day James and I met at the coffee shop was so perfect—almost like a scene out of a movie. Fate must have been on my side, because my hair was on point and there wasn't even a cloud in the crisp, clear December sky. The coffee was strong, and I can still remember feeling especially awake, with clarity for miles. The sun had just made its way over the shortest building that lined the humble downtown skyline and was pouring in through the wall-to-wall windows. I sat alone at a round, wooden table in the corner farthest from the door—my usual spot, arguably the best spot in the house. To my immediate left stood a narrow stainless-steel caddy that held the creams, sugars, honey, and cinnamon. Very convenient. I also liked that *my* table had initials with hearts around them carved into it—good reading material for a slow morning. And finally, from where I sat, I had a clear visual on any patron entering the small coffeehouse before they even reached the wood-framed glass doors.

I had arrived just after they opened that frigid morning, claiming the freshest cup of coffee possible and my favorite seat. Along with my writer's block, I was accompanied by a copy of J. D. Salinger's *The Catcher in the Rye* for inspiration and my composition notebook, which I carried almost everywhere back then. Holding a black pen loosely in my hand, I drew circles over and over until the paper bled, stopping only to take sips of coffee. My hand froze completely, however, when I saw him walk past the stretch of windows, heading straight toward the double doors. He was tall and muscular but not the gym-rat type, more like the "lumbersexual" look, with broad shoulders. His look was rough and unpolished, with a pair of dark fitted jeans and a hooded twill military jacket. His lush, dark hair was too long to be neatly pushed to the side, although it looked like he had tried, and his beard was thick but trimmed close so that it complemented his strong jawline. Serious eyebrows sat above his dark eyes, and just as I made note of his lips, he slightly grazed them with his tongue and pressed them together for short-lived relief from the wintry weather. He was all man and I was completely intoxicated by him.

He ordered a black coffee, of course, and sat alone in the corner opposite from me. I assumed he was waiting for someone, so I kept glancing toward the doors. But instead of acting as if he were expecting someone, he pulled a composition notebook of his own from a worn leather shoulder bag and began to write. I was dying to know the contents of that notebook. He seemed like the quiet type, one who might have better luck with a pen and paper than with saying things out loud. Lost in a daydream of dark sonnets that I imagined filled those pages, I caught myself staring dazedly at ancient water ring stains on my little round table, my pen no longer making contact with my paper. When I glanced his way, he was smiling—not at his writings but at me. Back then I would avoid an obvious gamble, but in his case I was willing to take my chances. Smiling back at him, I'm sure I looked innocent, but I didn't feel like it one bit; I thought about the words he was scribbling and then his pen and then his hand . . . I couldn't have looked away if I'd tried.

CHAPTER 3

AT FIRST SIGHT

JAMES

Never in a million years would I have ever approached her first. She was the kind of girl who made you want to stand taller and think quicker. Her green eyes commanded your attention, and once you made eye contact, it was all over. She was dainty without looking frail, and fit but not exactly athletic. Killer legs! Not long like the supermodel type but shapely as hell. She knew how to carry herself, that was for sure. And that smile . . . As approachable as that smile was, she could still make a man go weak in the knees.

The first time I saw Corinne she was sitting alone in a coffeehouse downtown. Even with her long wavy hair hanging over one eye, I noticed her looking in my direction. I thought maybe it was just the old, squeaking wooden doors opening and closing that had caught her attention, so I didn't think much of it. I ordered my usual and took a seat in the corner next to the windows; I could still feel her eyes on me. Man, this girl was anything but discreet . . . I liked it; more accurately, I was attracted to it. She was beautiful, which made it kind of hard not to stare back, so I pulled out a notebook and tried to focus on why I had gone there in the first place.

You might say that I got a little bit of a late start in the college scene; I was a twenty-eight-year-old junior at UNC Wilmington at that time, majoring in business with a minor in English. Christmas break was coming up, and I had a lot on my plate, and as an "adult student," I was probably a little more focused and determined than some of my classmates. In their defense, I guess a lot can change from twenty to twenty-eight. I had gone to the coffeehouse really early that morning to finish up an assignment. I'm pretty headstrong and nothing was going to distract me, not the glare of the sun in my eyes, not the howling wind seeping through the flaws in the wooden doors, and definitely not the gorgeous green-eyed girl sitting across the room.

I kept my head down, my textbook open, and I began to write. Aside from frequent breaks for refills, my eyes stayed true to my work. I didn't have a long list of accomplishments; due to my situation growing up, school had never really been a priority. When I was younger I'd gotten decent grades and even took an interest in classical music, but I hardly had time for school and we never had the money for lessons. Starting college felt like a second chance. Still, while my eyes concentrated on my assignment, which was now nearing fifteen pages long, I couldn't keep my thoughts from straying to the girl across the room. I considered a few options, one being that I would finish up my assignment, get a fresh refill, and head to class like planned; that idea was not my first pick. Another possibility was to walk across the room, slide into the empty chair at her table, introduce myself, and ask her out; much more action and confidence was involved in this scenario, which meant it was highly unlikely. Sometimes I wish I were *that guy*, but I'm not. The only thing I could actually see happening was that perhaps I could get a refill at the same time she did, and we would have to speak to one another. Maybe I would comment on the copy of *Catcher in the Rye* that was lying on her table or ask if she was a student—that was a legit question. Or I could ask her what she was working on in that notebook of hers; that could come across rude, though.

By this time my cup was almost empty, and I decided to steal a quick look in her direction. Her pen lay still in her hand as she stared at her notebook, like she was momentarily caught in a daydream. Her long blonde hair had fallen to the side, catching the sun rays that beamed in through the windows. She wore a cropped black denim jacket and a thick knitted red scarf wrapped cozily around her neck. Her tight jeans were tucked inside her short black lace-up boots. She was the perfect combination of cute and sexy. I was sure that a girl who looked like that would have a boyfriend. Hell, she could've had anyone. I took notice of her small, graceful hands; I admired her high cheekbones and how her pale lips were softly open, like she was concentrating. I wondered how she took her coffee and what her laugh sounded like. I wanted to know those things. I also wondered what she would think about me and my family, my upbringing. Or about the fact that I was a twenty-eight-year-old college student with nothing but an old black Jeep Wrangler to my name, along with thousands of dollars in school loans hanging over my head. I thought about all of the little details of our lives, pet peeves, and habits. I wondered what they would look like intertwined. Without warning, she broke away from her daze and her eyes immediately found their way to mine. The sun beamed across her porcelain skin and soft features; she was a vision. If there were ever such a thing as perfect, she was it.

CHAPTER 4

THE NIGHT CALL

It was three a.m. and the sound of the second hand ticking away on his stainless-steel watch seemed much louder than it should have. James sat in his bathroom on the edge of the tub, turning his phone over and over in his palm. He was unsure if it was really late at night or technically just really early. Either way, the house was silent and sound asleep, but he wasn't. He was wide awake, and his thoughts were running wild with possibilities.

The sound of his phone vibrating against his mirrored bedside table had woken him up at exactly 2:38 a.m. He didn't sleep very well these days anyway, so his reaction to the sound was immediate, and his attention had quickly turned toward the gentle humming near his head. He'd sat up and rubbed his eyes at the sight of the all-too-familiar name beaming on his phone as it continued to hum persistently. He silenced the vibrate setting and placed both feet on the plush carpet. His motions were agile and fluid as he eased out of the bed and slipped into the bathroom with his phone gripped in his hand. Careful not to make a sound, he closed the door behind him before switching on the light that hung above the oversize garden tub. The screen had gone black again. Now that he thought about it, he wasn't even sure if he would've answered the call or not if he were alone, but he desperately felt the need for a do-over, maybe even a do-over of the entire past year of his life. He concentrated on his phone, weighing the pros and cons of calling back, while praying it would light up one more time with that same name flashing across the screen. It never did.

He couldn't help but wonder what the hell Corinne was doing up this late, and he hoped she was okay; he prayed she was okay. It had been a year since the last time they'd *really* spoken, and that was just the two of them running into each other by chance at a concert. That night hadn't been ideal, since they'd both been on dates with other people. He was saddened at the thought that an entire year had passed by that quickly. He convinced himself that the late-night phone call was simply a pocket dial, that she was out with friends or maybe even on a date—probably the latter. Still, he couldn't shake the possibility that maybe she'd meant to call, maybe it wasn't an accident at all, and *maybe*, just maybe, there were things she wanted or needed to say. That thought alone hurt worse than her absence. He knew that even if he heard the words he had always hoped to hear, some things were undoable and time was a stubborn sea that waited for no one. Tides go in and out without faltering or permission, and that was just the way life worked. Everyone knew going back was not an option, but what if moving forward felt strangely off course?

James knew he didn't have the luxury of thinking that way anymore. A lot had happened over the last year. Who was he kidding—the last year had changed *everything* for him, and most days he could convince himself that it was all for the best.

Most days he was certain that everything happened for a reason, but today was not one of those days. Today he felt weak and lost in nostalgia. Today at three a.m. he sat in his bathroom in complete silence thinking about her and what could have been. He checked the time on his phone, cursing the fact that he had to be up for work in a few hours. For a moment he even considered calling her back just to be sure she wasn't in any kind of trouble. But before he could get very far with this thought, the bathroom door suddenly creaked open. James sat frozen with guilt and at a loss for words.

CHAPTER 5

THE MORNING AFTER, CONTINUED

Corinne began moving around the house, slowly but surely, and discovered her purse near the front door with her wallet unzipped and the contents scattered throughout. She started digging through the mess, hoping to recover her cell phone among the loose change, credit cards, and receipts from the bar. After a moment, she noticed her mint-green phone case with gold hearts peeking out from under the scarf that she had worn at the beginning of the night. Although it had completed her outfit, she'd had to lose the scarf after her third glass of merlot. Relief washed over her as she retrieved the phone. She made her way to her bathroom, mug and phone in tow.

Finishing off the last of her coffee, she sat the empty mug by the bathroom sink and leaned into the shower to turn the handle fully to the left. While the water was heating up, she took a deep breath and then took a seat on the closed lid of the commode and opened her list of recent calls. Right above her call to the Black Bird Taxi Company at 2:20 a.m. was James's name and number. The good news was, although she did call him at 2:38 a.m., the call lasted only for nineteen seconds, which meant he hadn't answered the phone.

"Oh, thank God." She laid her phone down on the edge of the sink, stripped out of her clothes, and hopped into the shower. The scorching hot water stung her skin a little but also felt cleansing; she needed some purifying after last night. Seconds after she started shampooing, she couldn't help but feel kind of sad that he hadn't answered. It had been a while since they'd last talked and even longer since she'd actually called him. She never could have imagined the day where she would call and he wouldn't answer. So what if she'd been under the influence at the time? The point was, he didn't answer and that was that. She instantly started to feel like a stereotypical, sappy girl, and she hated feeling like that. It turned out that even after all this time she was still a little lovesick when it came to him.

Corinne massaged a thick glob of cream rinse throughout her long hair. While she let the conditioner absorb, she eased her way to a seated position on her shower floor, bringing her knees up to her chest. Maybe it was all the caffeine, or perhaps she just needed something to eat, but she was beginning to feel a little lightheaded and weak. This feeling of heartache was a familiar and unwelcome one. A big part of her knew he had probably moved on, but it was the what-ifs that always left a glimpse of hope for her. For them. She was generally a happy person and pretty content; she would never admit to herself that she wasn't truly satisfied with her life. With one hand on the shower wall, she managed to pull herself to her feet and stood directly under the stream of water. She stayed this way with her eyes shut for a few minutes, trying to remember how she'd gotten here—what choices she had made or missed that brought her to this point, to this exact moment in her life.

Where her mind wandered to next seemed out of her control. She suddenly found herself back on that crowded terrace overlooking the Cape Fear River on New Year's Eve back in 2009, their first date. After grabbing a late dinner, they'd ended up at a masquerade party at a rooftop bar downtown. She and James were the only ones without disguises, their faces the only recognizable ones in the sea of masked individuals on the terrace. As the people shouted in unison, *"three, two, one,"* Corinne had lifted her champagne flute for a toast, but James had ignored the gesture and instead leaned in toward her. She gave in to him effortlessly. In a crowd of faceless strangers, it felt like they were the only ones on that rooftop as their lips met for the first time.

Trying not to dwell on that electrifying moment any longer, Corinne ran her fingers through her hair a few times. Once she was well rinsed, she turned the water off and reached for the towel hanging up just outside of the shower curtain. A thick fog filled the tiny bathroom. Not bothering to dry off first, she wrapped the towel around her body and tucked the corner piece, creating a dress-like cover. She could vaguely see the outline of her shape through the steam-covered mirror; she began to wipe away the condensation when something caught her attention out of the corner of her eye. Her phone had lit up. As if summoned by her thoughts, his name flashed on the screen.

CHAPTER 6

NEW YEAR'S EVE

WORK

In 2009, December 31 fell on a Thursday. Corinne was waiting tables on one of the most popular date nights of the year. This wasn't exactly her idea of a magical New Year's Eve, but the restaurant was pretty short staffed, and she hadn't requested the night off in time. In a college town on the biggest party night of the year, you had a couple of options: you ask off months in advance or you fake an illness and screw over the on-call person by forcing them to cover your shift, neither of which were options for Corinne. So she sucked it up and did the only thing she could do to make the night go by a little smoother and made a pit stop at Port City Java on her way in.

She pulled into the employee parking lot at four p.m., wearing her all-black attire and sipping on a primo nonfat honey latte. It was going to be a busy night full of multiple reservations, large parties, and plenty of "two tops"—restaurant lingo for a table for two. Before going in through the back kitchen entrance, she stopped outside the door to check her phone. That was also where almost everyone took their cigarette breaks, so the mulch area was littered with cigarette butts. No missed calls.

She entered the kitchen, made her way past the giant walk-in freezers and around the dish pit where a random fork lay dirty and abandoned, and finally glided through the dining room, surveying her second home. She headed straight for the front of the house to the small cabinet where she kept her personal items directly behind the hostess stand; this was where her beloved oversize designer purse would stay until the end of her shift. There was a possibility that the bag was a knock-off, considering Corinne's mom had bought it out of the trunk of an Oldsmobile in New York City. Either way, real or fake, the bag contained her life; tonight, the contents included a little green dress that she had purchased earlier in the day. She pulled the flirty green number out for a second to admire its cuteness.

"Just in case," she said, winking at the busboy as he came around the corner. He raised one eyebrow playfully and shook his head. Corinne was very popular in most circles she ran in. Her boss loved her because she could upsell to a filet mignon in less than two sentences, and her coworkers loved her because she didn't complain about sections or side work, she rarely found herself the center of gossip, and she was just fun and easy to get along with. And, of course, it didn't hurt that she was beautiful.

She tied her black apron tightly around her waist and slipped her cell phone into the large front pocket next to a few pens and straws. Over the next hour she cleaned her section, polished silverware, and constructed fancy cloth napkin folds.

By five p.m. she had her first table, and within thirty minutes the first dinner rush was in full swing and she was in her element, popping bottles of champagne and prosecco, toting oversize trays full of filets and salmon from the kitchen to the guests, and serving round after round of ritzy after-dinner drinks such as Drambuie and Grand Marnier. Raspberry cheesecake was the house special dessert for the night, and it was flying off the walk-in cooler shelves faster than you could say, "Would you all care for any dessert this evening?" If there was ever a time Corinne was happy to work in the restaurant industry, this was the night. Anything goes on New Year's Eve, from the nicest wines paired with crab and béarnaise-topped sirloin to Bailey's and coffee with their fifteen-dollar raspberry cheesecake. At seven thirty the first rush had begun to clear and she finally got a quick break. She went out the back door to where a few of her coworkers were enjoying a smoke. Corinne didn't smoke; she had a different kind of craving on the brain as she dug in her apron for her cell phone. She had a voice mail.

"Hey, it's James. So—I know you're working tonight, but I just wanted to let you know I might go ahead and just give this paper the rest of the night off. I'm feeling pretty good about it and I'd honestly like to see you . . . maybe when you get off work, if it's not too late. Hope to hear back from you. Happy New Year, Corinne."

There was a brief pause before he actually hung up, like maybe he had more to say.

She could hardly stand it. Her first reaction was literally jumping up and down—mostly out of giddiness, but also because she could have kicked herself for missing his call—and then she replayed the message . . . twice. It was torture for her. They had met a couple of weeks ago and exchanged numbers, but she hadn't really heard much from him; still, he was all she had thought about since. She wondered if he was *that* focused on his schoolwork or if he was just playing hard to get. She truly couldn't imagine him being the type that played games, but she also didn't have the most successful track record when it came to relationships and judgments of character. She wasn't a dumb blonde by any means; she was just very trusting and at times a bit naïve. A few days before, she had sent him a text, casually inquiring about his New Year's Eve plans, mostly out of curiosity, considering her plans consisted of serving lobster tails and filets to Wilmington's finest. He had responded immediately, telling her that his night was going to be equally productive and dull, as he needed to stay in to finish up a paper for school that was due the first week back from winter break. Still, he had made a point to say that he hoped they could hang out soon.

Although she'd been a little disappointed by his response, she actually thought pretty highly of his work ethic. She didn't know a ton of guys who cared that much about anything, let alone schoolwork, especially on New Year's Eve.

She was determined to see him tonight. She slipped her phone back into her apron pocket and walked back inside the kitchen area, only this time she took a hard left and headed straight for Robert's office. He was the manager and her only hope for getting out of this place at a decent time. Even if all that happened for New Year's 2010 was that she got to stand by James's side at midnight, she wouldn't complain. Robert said the best he could offer her was to cut her from the table seating rotation by ten p.m., which would put her leaving the restaurant by ten twenty if she hustled. She could work with that. Robert was a good guy and a great manager, and he really didn't like to say no to a hardworking employee.

Before reentering the dining room, Corinne stopped next to the dish pit and pulled out her phone to send James a text. He hadn't called that long ago, so hopefully he would get the message before he had time to commit to other plans for the night.

```
Hey there. Got your voice mail and I'd
like to see you too, only if you're
sure your paper could use the night
off. ;) Out of here by ten thirty.
Wanna meet . . . ?
```

She bit her lower lip and hit "Send" before thinking twice. He needed to respond quickly; another table in her section was probably being seated at this very moment, and she didn't want to go out there until he responded. The anticipation was almost painful, in that crazy-good kind of way. She tapped her foot, watched the second hand on the clock that hung above the coffeemaker, when suddenly, *ding*. She fumbled the phone in her loose, excited fingers. Her hands steadied again as she read the text.

```
I think my paper and I could both use
a night off. Meet you at your restau-
rant . . . looking forward to it.
```

"Yes!" she blurted aloud as she clutched her phone and pulled it to her chest. Dave, one of the other waiters, was passing through the kitchen and laughed at her while shaking his head. They had a casual, flirty friendship that was all in good fun and had been known to grab a drink with a few other coworkers after a shift. Although Dave may have had a crush on her at one point or another, he seemed to be content with their strictly platonic relationship.

"Someone's excited," Dave said playfully. "Big plans tonight, Corinne?"

"Oh, you know me, nothing too crazy," she responded.

She wanted to write something else back to James, but the hostess had just poked her head into the kitchen to let her know she had been seated with a party of six people. She didn't mind one bit; in fact, she was feeling recharged and ready for the rest of her shift. She put her phone back in the safety of her apron and with a smile plastered to her face she floated into the dining room.

CHAPTER 7

NEW YEAR'S EVE

PLAY

It was 10:03 p.m. when she officially clocked out. The second dinner rush had gone impossibly smoothly, and she hadn't had any more tables after nine p.m., which gave her plenty of time to fill up the ice bins, make a fresh pot of decaf for the late diners, and, with the help of Dave, polish twenty-five sets of silverware, all while still tending to her last two tables. The minute her final guests had paid, she grabbed her purse from the hostess stand and hurried through the bar area into the bathroom to freshen up.

Using the handicapped stall as her dressing room, she kicked off her nonslip uniform shoes and peeled down her fitted black pants, leaning her elbow against the wall to steady herself. Her purse hung wide open by one strap on the coat hook on the back of the stall door, the lacy hem of her dress peeking out. She began to unbutton her black collared work shirt and pulled it over the top of her head, slinging it over the door. She grabbed the dress, stepped into it, and had begun to zip it up when she remembered that the dress had a plunging neckline with a deep scoop on the back and hung off the shoulders. The bra she had worn to work that night was a pale-blue cotton T-shirt bra, and it was the only one she had with her. This was not going to work at all. Not wearing her new dress was simply not an option, so instead of stressing over what she couldn't change, she improvised. She took off the bra and finished zipping up her dress. She pulled out a pair of rose-gold suede heels and swapped them out for the black socks she had been wearing all night. They were pushing three inches tall, so she now stood about five four; she estimated that James was around six one, so he'd still have a solid seven inches on her. She balled up her uniform and shoved the mass, shoes included, into her giant purse and then exited the stall.

Setting her purse down on the counter next to the sink, she reached inside and dug around for her makeup bag. All she had in the striped canvas clutch was mascara, a cheek tint, and lip gloss; it wasn't much, but it would have to do. Luckily, her Minnie Mouse–like eyelashes naturally curled up to her brows. She brushed a second layer of mascara on to really darken them, highlighted the apples of her cheek with a rose tint, and then applied a smooth layer of clear gloss to her lips. Her lips were not her most standout feature, but, although they were thin, her top lip was perfectly defined and her bottom had just the right amount of poutiness that gave her a little sex appeal without a porno look. And just that like, she was ready, and the time on her phone read 10:12 p.m.

Exiting through the back door, she noticed how insanely chilly it was. The temperature had to be in the forties, easily. She tossed her purse in the trunk of her car and took a quick look around, hoping to find a sweater, but with no luck. She did, however, find her mint-green wristlet, which was perfectly suited for the occasion. She quickly stuffed her license and some cash inside, figuring that she'd go back in the restaurant for a drink at the bar, since she was about fifteen minutes early. She slammed the trunk shut and locked it with her key fob. When she turned to head back inside, she saw him. He was leaning against his black Jeep Wrangler, holding a small bouquet of pink tulips and wearing black boot-cut jeans with a white V-neck T-shirt and a black tailored-looking coat, unbuttoned, the collar standing tall. His dark hair was smoothed back, but a stray piece fell across his forehead. She didn't believe in love at first sight, but since this was their *second* encounter, she decided that this particular moment was an exception to that cliché.

It took him only a second to notice her, and when he saw her standing across the parking lot, he straightened his posture and stepped away from his car. Her stomach fluttered, and she smoothed her hands over the pleats in her dress as she walked toward him, the cold no longer seeming to have much of an effect on her. As she got closer to him, she could see him shifting from side to side. Feeling a little vulnerable, she dropped her eyes to the ground for a few paces, wishing she had a drink in her system already. When she looked back up at him, she was only feet away and his eyes were still locked unwaveringly on her. Now standing face-to-face, he smiled and took her by the hand, his other still grasped firmly around the pink tulips, looked her up and down indiscreetly, and then led her to the passenger side of his Jeep. His hand was calloused and rough but so warm as he held on to hers gently.

"I'm glad you were able to make it out tonight," he said. He opened the car door for her while still keeping his grip on the tulips.

Her hand still enclosed in his, she smiled, trying to appear cool and unaffected by his charm. "Well, lucky me that your assignment wanted the night off."

He winked and lifted the corner of his mouth into a half smile. "I might've wanted it a bit more." Like a gentleman, he helped her into his Jeep, using his forearm to slightly lift her so she could ease her way in. "These are for you," he said, handing the pink blooms to her. "I wasn't sure if you had a favorite flower or not, but for some reason these seemed like you." He looked toward the ground, but after a second he brought his eyes back to her.

"You must be *really* good, because tulips are my favorite." She smiled at the thought of him trying to figure her out. If this was the kind of thought he put into flowers, she could only imagine . . . "Thank you."

"You're welcome," he said just before he shut her door. The car must have been running the whole time while he was waiting for her, because it was toasty warm inside. It felt good and she could feel her shoulders loosen.

"So—where to?" she asked as he shut his door and got situated at the wheel.

"I thought you might be hungry after working all night, so I was thinking we could get some dinner."

He was gorgeous *and* considerate. With a hundred different ways to respond to him, words temporarily escaped her, and she just nodded and smiled. For some reason, she felt like he knew her, like he understood her . . . or, more importantly, like he wanted to. He politely nodded back and asked if she were warm enough. She said yes, but her arms had goose bumps, and he immediately took notice. He held his right hand against the vent for a few seconds to heat it up, then pressed his palm on her arm, letting his fingers wrap around her. She truly wasn't cold, but a chill went down her spine, causing her to shiver. The wide neckline fell loosely and draped off her left shoulder. He leaned over and with his left hand pushed the thin lacy strap back into place. He moved slowly, and she didn't move at all.

"Better?" he asked.

She was no longer chilled. In fact, she was feeling kind of hot. "Much."

"All right, well, if you don't mind me choosing, I know this place that serves dinner pretty late . . . you in?" he asked, raising his brows.

Dinner was the last thing on her mind. "I'm so in."

CHAPTER 8

MIDWEEK PLANS

It was a Wednesday and Corinne sat at her desk at the office watching the clock, waiting for five p.m. so she could finally leave work. She had been anxiously awaiting tonight ever since James had texted her on Sunday, making these last few days seem endless. Sitting in her old wheeled desk chair, she remembered Sunday afternoon; she pictured herself standing in her bathroom wrapped in her towel feeling slightly foolish, slightly hungover, and very confused. When she had opened the bathroom door leading to her bedroom, she was hit by a rush of cool air; she hadn't realized how comfortable she had become in the warm, steam-filled bathroom. Similarly, she had also forgotten how comfortable she had become in her everyday life until one simple gesture had changed everything and the butterflies had tangled her stomach into knots once again.

Unfortunately, she was convinced his text was simply in response to her drunk dial. His message had asked if they could talk, in person. She was fully prepared to explain herself by making light of the whole thing when he had texted again, asking if she would meet him on Wednesday night at The Bistro at eight. This caught her off guard, partly because they hadn't seen each other in well over a year, and also because she'd been expecting a much different reaction to the drunk dial. She'd assumed he'd be a little annoyed by a random call from her in the middle of the night, but so far he was proving her wrong.

Wednesday was a bit of a strange night to go out, but then again, it was half-priced wine night at The Bistro, which was nice. Although . . . she wouldn't want her thinking to be clouded by alcohol. She pictured the situation and decided that two glasses would be the right amount—enough to alleviate awkwardness without getting her too tipsy.

She had texted him back, with the intentions of keeping her reply light and relatively casual. "Hey there. Yeah, sure, that works for me. I was actually just about to text you . . ." Not quite as short as she meant for it to be.

All right, good. I'll see you then.

Wednesday was finally here, and at five p.m. on the dot she began closing up the office, turning off computers and lights, and locking the cashbox as well as the front door, being careful not to mention her evening plans to her coworkers as they all headed out the back door. They exchanged small talk about the changing seasons and how much they loved boots and pumpkin spice lattes, then went their separate ways. Corinne walked the short distance across the narrow parking lot to her car, kicking yellow leaves as she went. She drove a white Volkswagen Jetta that her parents had gotten her when she graduated from high school. They wanted her to have a safe and reliable vehicle for college, and the agreement was that if she got into college and worked a part-time job to cover gas, they would pay for her car. She had taken good care of it, and even though it was now ten years old, Corinne had no intentions of upgrading any time soon. It was paid off, and the insurance on it was affordable. Besides, she wasn't really a "car person." Fancy rides with shiny wheels and loud engines had never done anything for her. As long as it drove, then she was going to drive it.

It was 5:42 p.m. when she arrived home. She didn't live very far from her job, but the evening traffic in the small town made for an annoying stop-and-go commute. She lived in a little brick house painted white, with black shutters and a red front door. The red door is what initially drew her to the house, and she had quickly fallen in love with all its charm. It was small, but she didn't really need much space, since it was just Charlie and her. It was in a great old neighborhood with sidewalks, streetlamps, and nearby running trails. She stood on the tiny front stoop, fumbling through her purse in search of her key. A gust of wind blew, and more orange and yellow leaves began to fall, some landing in her purse and on her shoes. The beautiful tree that was shedding golden leaves across her yard was another selling point. It was truly magical looking.

Charlie was waiting for her inside the front door, as usual. She laid her keys on a small entry table and kneeled down to give him a bear hug and kisses before dashing into her bedroom to change into her workout clothes. Once changed, she headed back to the hall and grabbed Charlie's leash off the bronzed hook by the front door. She wasn't meeting James until eight, which meant she had plenty of time for a quick three-mile run. Charlie was getting older, but if not for the gray that speckled his nose and chin, you wouldn't be able to tell it—he could still keep up with her.

They took off out the front door, jogged to the end of the driveway, and turned left in unison, like it was a rehearsed dance routine. Once they reached the end of the street, they paused to check for cars, not missing a beat before crossing at the four-way stop. They took a running trail that veered off into the woods to the right and stayed on the path, following its course into the autumn wilderness. It was the most gorgeous trail, with tall pines that stayed true to their colors towering above the wooded skyline, crape myrtles bursting in vibrant oranges, and ruby leaves blanketing the beaten path. Like running on a sunset. It was a good place to unwind and get lost in your head and center yourself, just what Corinne needed before her "date" with James.

She and Charlie came back up the trail and onto the sidewalk, running at a much slower pace now, through the crosswalk and down the street to their home, where Corinne headed straight for the shower. While waiting for the water to heat up, she studied herself in the mirror: the light freckles across the bridge of her nose, the size of her breasts, a potential gray hair . . . (Luckily that last one was a false alarm; it was just a really blonde strand.) She wondered if she would look the same to him or different. Even though she didn't feel that different, a lot could change in a year. She hopped in the shower and carried out her usual routine, only this time she shaved her legs too, just in case. Grabbing a towel, she dried off quickly and wrapped the same towel around her hair; staying in the warmth of her bathroom, she moisturized from head to toe.

She unraveled the towel from her head, and while she allowed her wavy hair to air dry, she put on a little makeup, going for a very natural look, then painted her lips a soft shade of pink called "Nude Ballet." The pale-pink lipstick had just enough color to make her feel pretty without being too obvious.

As she opened the door from her bathroom to her bedroom, the cool air sent chills over her naked body. She went straight for her dresser and began to lay out all of the necessary items on her bed: underwear, bra, jeans, and a shirt. At first, she went for a plain, simple pair of cotton underwear. One reason being for comfort and the other being that of course nothing was going to happen between the two of them tonight so it wouldn't matter what her underwear looked like. After thinking it over, she reconsidered and picked out a thin black viscose pair she'd bought a few months back but hardly ever wore. She also selected a simple but sexy black balconette bra. It didn't have any padding; in fact, it was so sheer it was practically see-through, but it did have a nice push-up wire for a little more cleavage. Again, she told herself that there were no underlying reasons for her choice in undergarments. Her jeans were skinny and black, and her top was a thin chambray blouse that buttoned halfway down, leaving a tastefully plunging neckline. Standing in her closet, she debated which shoes to wear, overthinking it as usual. He was a tall guy so flats might make her feel like a little kid, but heels might imply she had gone the extra mile and thought this was a date. Minutes and multiple trials later, she decided on a black ankle boot with a small wedge heel. Her hair was almost completely dry when she rubbed three droplets of a richly scented Moroccan oil in the palm of her hands, then smoothed it through her loose curls.

She looked good.

The time read seven thirty on the Parisian-themed mantel clock as she paced back and forth in her living room, debating arriving early or on time. The Bistro was a fifteen-minute drive from her house, so she decided to use her spare minutes wisely and have a glass of wine instead. She retrieved a Bordeaux glass and filled it up halfway with a cheap but delicious red, then made her way back to the living room where Charlie was lying on the couch watching her every move. Taking a seat next to him, she relaxed her shoulders, took a deep breath and her first sip, and finally realized how nervous she was.

The last thing she wanted to do was to build up this night in her head, but she couldn't help it. He'd been a little standoff-ish in their recent texts, but no matter the details, it had been his idea to meet up. She finished the last sip of her wine and then set the empty glass down on the kitchen counter next to the sink and turned off the overhead sink light. Heading for the front door, she grabbed a cropped dark denim jacket just in case, and switched on a lamp in the foyer for Charlie. He lifted his head at the sound of her keys jingling but stayed snuggled on the couch. She stepped outside onto her little brick stoop and closed and locked the big red door behind her. Much to her surprise, it wasn't that cold out, so she folded the jacket over her arm and took the two steps down to her sidewalk while her hand lingered behind her on the old wrought-iron railing.

She felt good.

CHAPTER 9

THE BEGINNING

After their first official date on New Year's Eve, Corinne and James became inseparable, doing almost everything together. They ran together in the mornings, taking Charlie with them; James would stay overnight at her place after she got off work; they'd get coffee together and grocery shop together; they became best friends as quickly as they became lovers. Their chemistry was instantaneous, and their love developed much like a blazing wildfire in a drought. There was really no stopping it.

The spring of 2010 was perfect in Corinne's mind. James had just finished up school for the year and they enjoyed every second of his newfound carefree schedule. Corinne worked only in the evenings, so they spent their days at the beach, despite the cool weather that still lingered. James was an excellent surfer; Corinne, not so much, but they would head out early before the typical college summer crew could drag themselves out of bed and crowd the beaches. It was usually just the two of them and a morning jogger or two on the cool, windy beaches. With blankets and coffee in tow, wearing sweatshirts over their wetsuits, they watched the sun rise over the bright, blue-green Atlantic Ocean.

Early one morning, while they sat in the sand, and the breeze rolling in with the waves blew Corinne's hair in every direction, he pulled her closer to his chest, his breath warm against her neck. Gently, he pushed her wild hair out of her eyes and placed his soft lips so delicately on her forehead, warming her from the inside out. At times like these, they often said nothing at all. Words felt so insignificant in comparison to the moments they were sharing. Corinne was falling in love so hard, and it was evident in many ways that James was already there.

After weeks of these early coffee-and-surf sessions, Corinne eventually became a pretty decent surfer. He taught her how to paddle and how to stand up at just the right moment; timing was everything—that, and balance. After years of being a runner and building up her leg muscles, Corinne was naturally pretty steady, so they mostly focused on her timing. There were quite a few crash landings into the ocean that sent her board shooting through the waves, and as much as she hated saltwater in her eyes and up her nose, she wasn't keen on giving up either.

Most days, they'd spend an hour or so on the water, while the rest of the time they just talked, telling each other stories about their families and growing up and where they saw themselves in five years; jobs, families, and kids were all on the radar for both of them. James had always been a pretty intense guy, probably because he had to take life more seriously than most at an early age. While Corinne was playing soccer with friends after school, James was waking up at five a.m. in order to make it to work on time. It was a forty-five-minute walk one way for him, so he had to get an early start, especially if the weather wasn't cooperating that day. When he was working a fulltime job at minimum wage, his family could barely make ends meet, so James had decided to try his hand at construction. The pay was better, and he was picked up every morning and rode to the site with the crew, as opposed to his usual on-foot commute. He was nineteen at the time, strong and determined to learn, so he was a great candidate. He passed his drug test and was hired immediately. The hours were long and hard, but he learned a lot and got to physically and mentally exhaust himself every day, which helped with his stress-induced insomnia. Before the change in jobs, he had often found himself staring at the ceiling for countless hours, worrying over money, his younger siblings, and his mother. Once he got the construction job, he found falling asleep to be a little easier. The physical exhaustion as well as the pay increase eased his troubles. The only downside was that there wasn't any time left for him to explore his own passions. James had a fondness for music and an innate talent for playing the piano by ear. In middle school, he had spent any spare time he had in the music room, but those days were long gone now.

These stories made Corinne's heart hurt. She hated to think of him in such a hard place in his life, and hated even more that she couldn't relate to it at all. While he'd been pouring footings, laying brick, and putting on roofs, she was going to parties and the movies and having friends over on a weekly basis. She knew she'd had it easy growing up; she just never realized what a hard life consisted of until she met James. As he talked, she listened intently, taking in every word. He was truly opening up to her, and she could tell this wasn't something he did with just anyone.

Later that summer, Corinne was blindsided by news that no one could have prepared her for: her mom had been diagnosed with an advanced stage of cervical cancer, and extreme measures needed to be taken immediately. Because of her mom's very precarious condition, her father had to take an early retirement in order to take care of her. Her parents were young—only in their midforties—so the cancer and forced retirement had completely caught them off guard. Corinne's dad, Kevin, was the manager of a small construction firm, and although business had been slow that year, he'd had no intentions of calling it quits anytime soon. He was a worker; it was in his blood: his father was a worker, as was his grandfather. He was the kind of man who didn't know when to stop, and while it was admirable, it could also be unnerving. Corinne knew that even if he needed it, he would never ask for help—not with the business, not with the yard work, and certainly not when it came to the care of her sick mother. Kevin was like a machine; the only way he would ever stop was if he broke down. She worried over him almost as much as she did her mom.

Corinne wasn't used to turmoil or tragedy, especially not this close to home, so she didn't exactly know how to handle any of it. James tried to be there for her as much as possible, but she hardly knew how to let him. He encouraged her to get out of town and be home with her family, assuring her that he could help support her financially while she took time off work, but she found herself pulling away from him as opposed to leaning on him. In addition, her mother could be as stubborn as her daughter and would often talk Corinne out of coming home, insisting that she was fine. Corinne knew she was lying, but a small part of her wanted to believe it and wanted the reality of the sickness to be as distant as possible. That small part of Corinne wasn't something she was proud of, and she knew she needed to face reality eventually, but as long as her mom kept her at bay, she tried not to fight it. Instead of taking time away from work, she did the opposite and started picking up extra shifts. Most of them were closing shifts, keeping her at the restaurant until midnight or so. She stopped writing, and eventually her daily run with Charlie also came to a halt, because both hobbies required her to be alone with her thoughts, and that would mean she'd have to face everything she was scared of. She was pretending to be fine all of the time, and pulling it off less than half of the time, but it was getting old. James wasn't blind; he could see she was in a dark place.

One night after she had already gone to bed, he pulled into her driveway. It was unusual that he wasn't there with her already, spending the night with her, but she had worked the closing shift and wasn't particularly feeling up to company.

He had his own key to her place, so he quietly let himself in through the front door, gripping the keys carefully, making sure not to jingle them. Luckily, Charlie was used to James letting himself in and didn't bark, instead greeting him with a wagging tail. James let Charlie lick the side of his face and patted him on the back, then made his way to Corinne's bedroom. Her door was slightly ajar. The floors creaked under his feet as he stopped outside of her room and pushed the door open with his fingertip. As he neared the side of her bed, he looked at her sleeping so soundly; he hadn't seen her look this serene in weeks. She let out a sigh in her sleep just as he leaned over her delicate body and wrapped one arm around her shoulders and the other under her legs and lifted her from underneath her mountain of covers and held her closely. She instinctively held on to him, nuzzling her face against his chest. When she opened her eyes it took her a second to go from happy to surprised to confused.

"What are you doing here? What time is it?"

"It's okay, it's okay, I promise," he assured her. "Baby, I'm so sorry I woke you up, but I have something I need to show you."

The confusion had fully set in now, along with nervous-ness. "Okay . . ." she said. "Are you sure you're okay?"

He smiled at her with such love and admiration in his eyes, and with a very convincing tone said, "I'm good, baby. You don't ever have to worry about me."

He carried her out of her room and set her down on her feet in the foyer. She was wearing an old white T-shirt and faded black sweatpants that had been cut into a pair of shorts. He grabbed a light jacket hanging by the door and handed it to her, and with a puzzled look she asked, "Are we going somewhere?"

Charlie perked his head up from where he had settled on the couch and watched the commotion going on by the front door. James walked back into her bedroom and returned with a pair of worn leather flip-flops.

"Put these on too," he said.

She slipped her feet into her flops, all the while keeping her eyes on him and waiting for an explanation. She didn't get one; instead he grabbed her hand and guided her out the front door, then used his key to lock it up behind them. He led her to his Jeep and opened the door for her as he always did, then ran around to the driver's side. The windows were down; the air was warm and sweet, and the crickets played exuberantly as he started the engine. He looked at Corinne. Her eyebrows were raised in confusion, but she had a smile spread across her face.

"Where in the world are we going?" She laughed.

"Mad, baby, we're going mad." His eyes were wild and full of excitement. She threw her head back, letting out a genuine gush of laughter, feeling the lightest she had felt in weeks. James wasn't the comedic type, but he had his moments. He usually had no intention of being funny; he just said what he thought, and sometimes he was being serious and other times he was quoting one of his favorite authors, but it always seemed to fall into place perfectly. Hearing her laugh made him smile.

He leaned over the armrest between them, placed one hand behind her neck, and gently pulled her toward him. He kissed her once on her forehead and lingered for a moment before he sat back in his seat and just looked at her. She grabbed his hand and he squeezed hers back. Using his left hand, he put his Jeep into "Drive" and then pulled out of her driveway.

It was a quick trip to the beach, less than ten minutes, and Corinne held her right hand out of the window the whole time, periodically switching her gaze from the scenery to James and then back again, but his eyes never left the road. He almost seemed nervous. After they crossed over the bridge, the beach was less than three miles away, and within minutes he pulled down Lumina Avenue and parked within walking distance of the pier. Before getting out of the car, he leaned into the backseat and grabbed a blanket, a telescope, and a small package wrapped in a thick brown kraft paper. Without saying a word, he walked around to her door. She was already opening it, and he hurriedly took her by the hand. He led her down a narrow path of beach grass and sand until the grass faded away and the sand became too deep to comfortably walk in with shoes. She kicked off her flip-flops and carried them until she and James were just a few feet away from the ocean. The waves seemed incredibly soft and gentle, and it was a clear night with a large moon. The sound of the waves breaking against the shore made her feel at ease; she closed her eyes and stood facing the water for a moment until he interrupted her by wrapping his arms around her from behind. She took a deep breath in, and he held her a little tighter.

When Corinne opened her eyes, James was turning her around to face him, showing her where he had laid a thick, soft blanket on the sand next to them. He started to sit, lightly pulling on her hand so she would join him. As they got situated, he brought the telescope out from behind him and pulled a small folded sheet of paper from his back pocket. He unfolded and studied the paper while she studied him; his eyebrows were furrowed, and he slightly licked his lower lip in concentration, every now and then saying something under his breath like he was trying to solve a word problem.

"You need some help?" she asked. He shushed her and she giggled, covering her mouth in an attempt to be discreet. A minute had passed when he finally looked back at her and smiled.

"Are you ready?" he asked her, like she was about to blow out the candles to make a birthday wish.

She laughed at him again, louder this time, not even trying to hide it. "Ready for what, crazy?"

He took a peek through the telescope and made one final adjustment to the sight, then pulled her gently by the arm. Instead of asking questions, she humored him by leaning in and taking the telescope into her hands and pressing her eye against the eyepiece. He laid the unfolded sheet of paper in front of her and started to describe what she was looking at through the small, high-powered lens. It was the Hercules constellation, he explained. She pulled back from the telescope and looked at him, unsure what to think at this point; he continued to tell her about the constellation's history and the number of stars that made it up. She leaned back in for another look. This time she didn't look away from the sky again until he stopped speaking and handed her a small rectangular package. It was neatly wrapped in a heavy-duty brown paper with thin yellow yarn tied around it in a messy bow. He held the small gift very carefully in his large, strong hands, as if it were an injured bird. She cautiously took it and started to unwrap it. When she did, she found a piece of paper in a black distressed wooden frame. It was a small map of the Hercules constellation along with a formal printed certificate. The certificate read:

LET IT BE KNOWN TO ALL THAT THE STAR
DESIGNATED IN THE SCIENTIFICALLY RENOWNED
STAR CATALOG AS *Kornephoros, Beta Herculis*
AND RESIDING WITHIN THE BOUNDARIES OF THE
CONSTELLATION HERCULES, "THE BRIGHTEST
STAR" IS HEREBY NAMED IN HONOR OF LAURIE
ELAINE DAVIS.

Her eyes began to fill with tears before she could even say anything; she sat in silence for a moment trying to think of words, but nothing would come out. She felt her face beginning to flush hot with blood and emotions, and the sensation spread across her whole body, causing chill bumps on her bare legs. She squeezed the wooden edges of the frame and bit her lip trying to keep from crying, but the tears came, at first just one that landed on the glass in the center of the diagram, and then a hundred more. James started to put his arms around her, but she leaned away from him, still saying nothing. Ignoring her body language, he grabbed her by the arms and held her tightly. She hit his chest with her fist, trying to resist his embrace, but he didn't falter and he didn't let her go. Only a few seconds had passed when she collapsed into his arms, letting his body blanket hers, and neither one of them changed positions for what seemed like forever. When she finally sat up to look at him, all she could see in his dark eyes was what she was feeling herself: love; love like she didn't know could exist, love like she didn't think she even deserved.

"You're strong and brilliant, just like your mom, Corinne, and just like this star. This is in her honor. This is for you." His gaze was steady. "Corinne, I—"

"I love you," she interjected, between breathy sobs. "I love your heart and your mind; I love your hands and your mouth. I love you so much that sometimes I can't even believe that this is real life, that we found each other in this world and that we have *this*; this is everything . . . You are everything, James."

He had never been in love before until her. The sound of it, the feel of it, the taste of it—everything was new and it made him feel so alive. As she sat there looking at him with her glossy green eyes, sniffling and almost shaking, he realized he loved her in a way that couldn't be described by words. He leaned closer to her, holding her head in his hands, his thumbs against her rosy cheeks. His breathing was deep and more rapid than usual; he couldn't get enough of her. Their foreheads pressed together for a moment, and with a slow, consuming intensity, his lips met hers, partially opened, just grazing them at first. Then, completely giving in to him, she twisted her hands into his thick, smooth hair, holding on to him like a lifeline. Moving one hand down to the small of her back, he lowered her onto the velvety blanket spread across the sand, keeping his body weight off her. But she pulled him down against her chest, wanting to feel the movements of his breathing. Although they had known before this point that they were falling in love, this was the moment they knew for certain that some fires burned hotter than others. His lips lingered against her ear as he whispered, "I love you too, Corinne."

CHAPTER 10

CONFESSIONS

CORINNE

When I arrived at The Bistro for the Wednesday night "date" with James, the parking lot was almost empty, just as I imagined it would be. I pulled into the first spot I found and looked around for his Jeep. I wasn't even sure if he still drove it, but that's the vehicle I often found myself doing a double take for around town. I didn't see it, so I locked up my VW and decided to grab a table and a drink while I waited. It was cozy and dimly lit inside, with tea lights decorating the tables. Black-and-white photos of North Carolina's lighthouses lined the walls. The setting was vintage and chic, just the way I like it. The song playing in the background was by Death Cab for Cutie, and it immediately took me back to a few years prior, my last encounter with James; the universe is cute that way.

My thoughts were interrupted when someone put their hands on my shoulders from behind. At first it made me jump, but then my whole body relaxed. I could smell his scent, which hadn't changed a bit; his hands were warm and rough on my skin, his touch firm and steady. He stepped around to meet me face-to-face, and his hands lingered on my neck for a moment.

"Miss Davis, you have not changed a bit. I thought I saw you pulling in ahead of me on two tires, hitting the curb," he joked playfully. "You still drive the Volkswagen?"

He had jumped right in like we were old friends; I guess we technically were? "Of course I do. That car gets better with age." *That's fine, I can be friendly.*

"I think you mean wine." He smirked.

"No, well, yeah, that too. But my car is totally aging well." I refused to get tongue-tied, but it was easy to do in his presence.

"Kinda like us, huh?"

"If by us you mean me, then absolutely." He let out a cute laugh that made me smile more naturally.

He seemed more at ease in person than he had via text. He placed his hand on the small of my back and gestured toward a table. There was no hostess tonight, Wednesdays not being a busy night. There were two other couples dining and two girls sitting at the bar together, taking advantage of the half-priced wine special. We sat at a table along the wall near the back of the room. You could see almost the entirety of the restaurant from one angle, with the exception of the bar, which was off to the side, a dark screened partition separating it from the main room.

The waiter came to get our drink orders first. I peeked at James from behind the menu and waited a second to see what kind of night this was going to be. He seemed to be mulling it over before deciding on a whiskey and soda on the rocks. I raised my brows in agreement and the waiter then directed his attention to me.

He was a young guy, maybe a few years younger than me, and actually pretty attractive. I wondered if he assumed James and I were together. *Who knows, this guy could totally want to ask me out but he thinks I'm unavailable because here we are, sitting together, just the two of us on a random Wednesday night, like this is something we do, just go out for whiskey and half-priced wine.* The waiter was definitely checking me out, but in a subtle way to be respectful. I could be missing out on a potential dating prospect by being here with James.

"I'll have a glass of merlot, please . . ." I dragged out the ending in "please" while I strained to read the name on his shirt, "Brad."

There was way too much product in his hair, and his cologne was suffocating me. Maybe there wasn't a future for me and Brad. He left to get our drinks from the bar, and then it was just us again.

"So . . . How have you been?" James asked. It was a simple question; I was relieved we were going to be starting out slow.

"Good, really good. Just working, still running with Charlie, Ava still harasses me about moving back home; I still see her and Andrew every couple of weeks when I make the trip. Sometimes I'll stay with them when I visit so that gets her off my back for a bit . . ."

"Your sister is something else" was all he had to say about that. Ava was never exactly "team James," and he'd always felt like she was trying to control or influence me, even from three hours away. It was hard to get mad at her, though. Even though she was my little sister, she had a very mothering personality and always believed that she truly knew what was best for me. She thought she was doing me a favor.

"I miss that dog, Charlie-bear." He grinned. "How's he doing? He must be getting up there. You've had him for a long time now."

"I know, I know. He's nine now, but he can still keep up." I smiled pleasantly. This was a bunch of small talk and it was killing me. "Hey, so I'm guessing you saw that I called you last weekend kinda late one night."

"I did. I was going to ask you about that. I'm sorry I didn't answer; I was passed out pretty hard." I couldn't tell if he was being honest or not. "You must have been out pretty late, huh?" He said it like a joke, but I knew it was a real question coming from him.

"Yeah, about that . . . I'm so sorry. No good reason, I guess, just wanted to say hi." I shrugged and smiled innocently.

"At three a.m.?" He smiled back with a more mischievous grin.

"Yep, at three a.m. Why put off till tomorrow what you can do when you're drunk?"

He let out a genuine laugh, tilting his head back and looking at the ceiling as if he were collecting his thoughts. "Oh man, you have always been the funny one." He looked sincere. "I've missed this." His eyes fully focused on me. "Are you still writing?" Brad was tableside dropping our drinks off. James thanked him then directed his attention right back to me and raised his glass. "To us?"

"To us," I confirmed and our glasses clinked. My muscles tightened.

"So back to you . . . You're still writing, I hope," he said.

"Some. Definitely not as much as I used to or would like to, but I guess that's what happens when you start working full-time." My answer was lame and so not me.

"Right, right . . ." He seemed unconvinced. "And are you happy?"

60

He was asking for the truth, and he was the last person I wanted to lie to. "Honestly, a piece of me feels like it's missing. My job is fine; it's a good job, but it doesn't fulfill me or challenge me at all. Sometimes I pull in the parking lot and think about just pulling right back out." And that was the truth. He seemed to believe this answer much more than the one before.

"You know you're insanely talented, don't you?" he said. "I mean you really are, Corinne. You have a way with words like writers from way before your time, and the way you always carried a pocket thesaurus around was very strange but also very charming." His whole face was smiling. "It's who you are, you know? I just don't want you to lose that."

Staring at the floral print on my napkin, I nodded. No one had talked to me like that in years. No one had known me like he had—like he does. A part of me wanted to thank him for saying those things to me, and an even bigger part of me wanted to cry because all this was coming from the mouth of the man I should be with but wasn't. We were simply having dinner together, or at least I thought we were.

Brad approached the table again to take our orders. James and I quickly agreed to split a basil-and-mozzarella flatbread and get another round of drinks, even though our current glasses were only half empty.

The conversation got much lighter from there, and we ended up talking for hours. He told me about the job he landed with the university last fall as a part-time student advisor and counselor, working his way into the classroom. We discussed books and music, gushing over our favorites and sharing them with each other, and reminisced about our time together— only the good stories, though. The conversation got a bit heavy again when he asked about my mom.

She had been battling cervical cancer for just over four years now. The news had been a complete shock to me, seeing as nothing had ever been wrong with her before, as far as I knew. She seemed fine during our daily talks on the phone or when I was home visiting them. I had no idea what she had been keeping from me—from everyone. My dad had known something was going on with her and had tried his hardest to convince her to see a doctor for over six months. Apparently Christmas of 2009 was when she started noticing some things about her body; it started out as pain in her abdomen, which she wrote off as a stomach bug, despite its intensity. The next big sign was her menstrual cycle; she and I were close, and I couldn't help but notice that when I was home visiting, it always seemed she was on her period. I asked her about it one time, pointing out that the last time I was home we'd been on the same cycle, and I wasn't expecting mine for another two weeks. She made a joke about menopause, and it was never brought up again. My mom was forty-four at the time, so the idea of menopause seemed a little early, but I didn't push it. I didn't know if something like cancer in my family seemed impossible, or if it was just me being naïve—I guess the two go hand in hand—but I regret my nonchalance about the whole thing.

They began her treatment with some pretty hard-hitting chemotherapy and radiation, and she was much sicker than she let on. I was waiting tables at the time, and my boss was more than understanding about all the time I was taking off. In fact, they kind of just "held" my position there for whenever I was in town and available to work. I was incredibly grateful.

James was also super supportive. He never once questioned me or my timing when I felt like I needed to go home; even if it was in the middle of the night, he would brew a tumbler full of coffee for my three-hour drive and fill my car up with gas while I was throwing my stuff in a bag. And even though we had known each other only for about six months when all of this began, he made a few of those trips home with me.

"She's doing well for the most part," I said when he asked about her now. "Just taking it one day at a time . . . She's really tough, you know?" It was the kind of vague answer you perfect when you have a sick family member; no details, no deep truths or confessions, always speaking to the strength and character of your sick loved one and staying positive. No one ever knows what to do with the honest truth, anyway.

"She is tough, I know that firsthand." He smiled. "But you don't have to give me a line you've rehearsed. I asked because I really care, Corinne."

He seemed so genuine it made me want to cry a little, but I couldn't help but think about how he had stopped checking in and asking about her over a year ago. Did he *really* care then too? While I didn't expect him to live his life wrapped up in the past, it wouldn't have killed him to call or text. I knew I was being overly sensitive, though. It definitely wasn't his responsibility to check in on me or my family. And he was here asking me now. That said enough.

"I know . . . you're right. It's a habit I've formed to ward off pity looks and 'it's God's plan' speeches. The truth is, she is okay. She had a hysterectomy in March, and, although the doctors say it was a successful surgery, she's been having some other complications related to the surgery ever since. It's been hard, especially on my dad, and I feel bad that I'm not there more . . . definitely not as much as my sister."

"Oh wow, I'm so sorry." He shook his head. "But I know you do the best you can. I mean, you're three hours away with a job and a dog, and it would be crazy to pretend like it's *easy* to just take off."

"Well, I know I could do better, and you telling me I'm doing the best I can makes me feel kind of guilty," I said. "Like you're making excuses for me." I truly didn't mean to come across as critical, but I must have looked a little pissed off.

"Whoa, whoa, Corinne. I wasn't trying to make you feel bad. I just wanted you to know that I'm sure your parents understand, that's all. Of course Ava is able to be there more; she lives five minutes away from them. Just don't be so hard on yourself."

I wasn't mad at James; I was mad at myself. I really didn't have a good reason not to be back home. Sure, I had a few friends from college still around town and an okay job, but I knew that wasn't why I was here. Part of me believed that as long as neither James nor I ever left Wilmington, there was a definite chance that we would reconnect. It wasn't something I was actively pursuing, but I thought fate might have better luck if I stayed local. Take tonight, for example. Maybe a drunk dial was what was going to get the ball rolling. It was a selfish thought, and it made me feel guilty. James was staring at me as if trying to figure out what was going on in my head. I loved his eyes on me but was very glad he couldn't read my mind.

"Let's talk about you. I'm starting to get bored with myself." I straightened my posture and leaned in, propping my elbows on the table. "What's new with you besides work? Seeing any-one these days?" Half kidding, half being nosy. He paused as if searching for the words.

"I am . . . actually. Since earlier this year." He said it very matter-of-factly, as if that would make it seem like less inter-esting news.

"Oh. So is it, like, serious?" I tried my hardest to sound more curious than heartbroken.

"Kinda, well, yeah—I guess it is pretty serious. We moved in together, actually . . . this past spring."

He looked nervous, which made me uneasy. Why was all this just coming up now, and why did he look so freaking nervous? He picked up his glass, finished the last sip of his drink, and swirled a few pieces of ice around in the bottom.

"Okay—so you live with someone? I'd say that's pretty serious. Was it your idea? Just curious. I mean, it's fine, it just seems kinda soon to take it to that level . . . ?" I didn't want to come off as judgmental, so I focused on playing up the concerned friend role. Just looking out for him, that's all.

"Well, we met last September, but I guess we technically got together earlier this year . . . and . . . I was the one who suggested she move in . . ." There was a long pause; it was like we were both seeing who would go next. Finally, he took a deep breath, signaling he had something else to say. "She's . . . I mean I—I wanted to tell you that we . . . She's pregnant, we are . . . we're having a baby."

I smiled weakly, but it was all I had in me as my vision started to blur. I knew I had to keep from crying. I blinked quickly, and a tear fell from the corner of my eye. He looked down at his hands for a second, pretending not to see the tear, while I quickly swiped it away with my finger. My stomach tightened and my face burned hot; I could only imagine the coloring of my cheeks as I began feeling lightheaded. He continued to stare at his lap, not wanting to look me in the eye. I wanted to look away from him too, but for some reason I couldn't. He looked like my old boyfriend and sounded like my old boyfriend, but something was different about this guy. This man appeared to be scared, his hands seemed unsteady, and his skin looked pale and flushed, almost like he was going to be sick. I could easily relate.

CHAPTER 11

THE BEGINNING
OF THE END

It was the early spring of 2011, and the weather still called for jackets and the flowers hadn't yet blossomed. Corinne's mom, Laurie, was actually doing really well; the doctors were hopeful that she would be in remission before the end of the year. For James, school was still in session, and in a little less than two months he would graduate from UNCW with his degree in business. This was a big deal to him; he was the first in his family to ever attend college, and the fact that he was about to graduate *and* was on the dean's list was quite an accomplishment.

Corinne waited outside of his last class so they could get a late lunch together before she went to work for the night. She usually needed to be at work by four p.m. to get ready for the dinner crowd, and it was already almost three now. She was going back and forth between checking her phone and checking the front door to the building where his classes were held.

They were supposed to meet outside of this exact building at this very water fountain at two thirty, she was positive. She sent him a text message, hoping she just had the wrong building, but he didn't respond. After a few minutes a girl came out carrying a backpack that looked like it weighed more than she did. Corinne took a chance and asked her if she might know an older student in the business program. She described him first, then mentioned his name.

"Oh yeah, I know James!" the girl said. "He is *so* sweet! We have two classes together on Thursdays. You actually just missed him."

Corinne smiled, amused by the young girl's response. "Do you happen to know which direction he went? I was supposed to meet him thirty minutes ago, and I can't get him on his cell."

The girl's mouth dropped open as if she had an aha moment. "Oh! You're his girlfriend . . . Corinne, right? Aww, he loves you so much." She giggled. Corinne never really thought of herself as old, but this girl was kind of making her feel that way.

Corinne fake laughed, trying to sound polite as she asked the girl again if she had seen where he went after class.

"He's probably in the music building. Sometimes he goes over there if class lets out a little early."

Corinne thanked the girl and turned to head in that direction. She couldn't help but feel slightly irritated at the whole situation; he wasn't where he said he would be, he wasn't answering her texts or calls, and that girl in his classes was sweet but had also annoyed her for some reason. The music building was just on the other side of the library, so she made it there quickly and decided to take a look inside to see if he was around. It was highly unlikely that he would just forget plans with her, so maybe she'd gotten his class schedule wrong. She pushed open the large wooden door to the old building. It let out a loud creak that echoed in the empty hall. She stopped and stood still, waiting to hear voices, but no sound came. She stepped inside and looked around. There were multiple halls branching out from the front room like spider legs. She heard something; it sounded kind of far off, a piano being played.

With light footsteps, she started down the hall straight ahead of her. The piano began to get louder, until soon she felt like it could be behind any door. She glanced down at her phone to see if she had heard anything from James yet; nothing at all, so she started looking through the small slit of glass on each door. The first two rooms were dark and empty, but when she turned to her left she noticed that the next door coming up had light shining through the window. She moved closer and looked inside. James was sitting at a baby grand piano, playing wildly. His eyes were shut, as if he were performing his emotions instead of an actual musical piece. He was so beautiful, and the music was so beautiful, that for a moment she didn't even want to interrupt, but her phone alarm buzzed, reminding her that she needed to be at work in less than an hour.

A small part of her felt a little jealous of the piano. His hands on the keys, his lips pressed together in complete concentration; heart and soul were written all over him. She knew he was focused on school, and many times it came first, but this didn't really fall in that category. This wasn't something driven by determination, this was love. This was his *other* love, the love that came before Corinne. Forgetting his date with her may have seemed like an innocent mistake, a single random instance, but to her it felt like more than that; it felt like this was a glimpse of where his heart was, and it felt like he was slipping away. The last few weeks he had seemed distracted. He always blamed it on school-related stress, and she usually believed him. Not that he was lying to her, but sometimes the easiest thing to do when you can't quite figure out where your head is was to place blame on the obvious. She couldn't help but wonder if there were something more to his recent half-heartedness toward her. The possibility of a "rough patch" had recently crossed her mind, but they had never seemed like the kind of couple that grew tired of one another's company or "needed space."

The alarm on her phone buzzed again with another work reminder; this time she turned it off instead of hitting "Ignore." She turned away from the door, the music, and her man, and headed down the hall back to the front doors. Unsure if her feelings should be hurt or not, she decided to leave the situation alone and make nothing of it; instead of playing the victim, she walked through campus to her car and went straight to work.

She got there early enough to have a quick salad before starting her shift, and although she didn't want to, she couldn't help but check her phone repeatedly as she ate. Nothing. At four p.m. on the dot, she walked out of the restroom after changing into her uniform, tucking a few loose strands of hair behind her ear; she pulled her cell phone out one last time before filling up the ice stations and water pitchers and discovered she had two missed phone calls and a voice mail. She was relieved to see his name next to the missed calls but also a little irritated that he knew she would be at work now, so she decided it wouldn't kill him to wait like she had. Before the last water pitcher was filled, she got her first table of the night, a party of six. She was glad to be busy; she could definitely use the money and the distraction.

It was a weeknight, so things really slowed down by eight p.m., and Corinne clocked out forty-five minutes later. She pushed open the exit door in the back of the kitchen and checked her phone while she walked to her car. There was another missed call and one text message. It was from James: "I tried calling you."

She'd honestly thought he might say a little more than that. Maybe even an "I'm sorry." As she started through the parking lot, her eyes still fixed on her phone, she debated what to text back, or whether she should just call him. Or maybe she should listen to the voice mail? Her thoughts were suddenly interrupted when she looked toward her car and saw James standing outside of his Jeep, parked right beside hers. The sight of him made her stomach tighten a little. Seeing him always did that to her; this time, however, she was actually a little nervous.

He was wearing his staple white V-neck T-shirt and dark jeans and was holding a bouquet of yellow tulips, which were practically glowing they were so bright. Before she could reach him, he walked toward her, meeting her halfway. She tried to think of something clever to say, but before she could say anything at all he wrapped both arms around her, pulling her against his chest; his whole body hugged hers like a warm coat, and she felt the flowers pressed against her hair. She hadn't been upset because he was late, or that he even forgot—sure, those things had definitely hurt her feelings—but it was the culmination of everything from the past few weeks building up that made her feel insignificant, which was not a feeling she was used to, not with James.

It had all started two weeks ago, on a Saturday evening that had begun like most of their weekends together. Corinne was working and James was supposed to meet her at her place when she finished for wine and indie films, as usual. She called him on her way home from the restaurant, but he hadn't answered. She sent him a text message when she got home, letting him know that she was there. She went ahead and let Charlie out to relieve himself, changed into some sweatpants and a tank top, and opened up a bottle of wine. Starting to become a little worried, she was about to call again when he texted her, letting her know that he was really tired and wouldn't be coming over.

Corinne had been a little surprised. Not that he was tired, she could understand that, but who was too tired for a movie on the couch? Instead of starting an argument over something so petty, she decided to let it go and had a glass of wine in the company of her dog, then called it a night. The very next week, they had plans to meet up at his apartment after she got off work to go to a birthday party downtown. The party was for a good friend of James's who was turning thirty; he and his girl-friend had rented out a local bar called Goodfella's. Corinne clocked out at eight p.m. and had her stuff with her. On her way to his apartment she called to let him know she would be there in just a few minutes, but he didn't answer. When she pulled up to his building she noticed his car wasn't there, so she dug through her purse to find her phone. She saw she had a missed call and a voice mail from just a few minutes before. She had forgotten to take her phone off silent after leaving work. The voice mail was from James, except she could hardly hear him over all the music and commotion in the background.

> *"Hey, it's me. I actually went ahead downtown with the guys, so just meet me—"* There was a break in the message where he started talking to someone else at the bar, followed by some laughing. *"Hey, sorry. Meet me down here, okay?"*

Click.

Remembering these recent incidents made Corinne feel sick to her stomach as she stood in the parking lot of the restaurant, James holding her tightly. It wasn't that any of this was really *wrong*; there was no cheating or lying involved, but it was insensitive and inconsiderate and just so not them. Neither one of them said anything right away, just silence as she felt his

72

lips on the top of her head. He took a deep breath, and when he exhaled all he said was "I'm so sorry." Even though they both knew apologies wouldn't fix anything, at that moment it was all she needed to hear.

CHAPTER 12

OLD HABITS DIE HARD

Even years after their breakup, it seemed like timing was still not on their side. Corinne drove home in silence, trying to process the news of James being an expectant father. Their "date" at The Bistro had proved to be more informative than she had ever imagined. She went over the entire dinner in her head, asking herself a million questions that she hadn't had the nerve or clarity to ask him: Who was this woman? Did he love her? Were they going to get married? She wished more than anything she'd had the guts to ask him all these things, but the shock of the news had left her wanting to flee the scene rather than get deeper into it.

After he told her about the pregnancy, she had wasted no time in downing her half-full wineglass as quickly as possible and signaling Brad for the bill. James hadn't moved or touched his drink. The cubes in his whiskey clinked as they melted and shifted in his glass, but he'd sat motionless, seemingly unsure of what to say to make the situation better, or at least easier. He was still searching for the right words when Brad approached the table with his easy-come, easy-go swagger. Corinne had both envied and hated him for a moment. He laid one joint ticket on the table and James pulled out his wallet, but Corinne had already slid the ticket her way and had cash in hand. James tried to convince her to give him the bill while handing his credit card to Brad. She unwaveringly refused and shoved a wad of cash, which included a very large tip, in Brad's direction. He looked uncomfortable but took the money and hesitated for a second, looking back and forth between the faux couple. Before he could say anything, Corinne said, "Keep the change" and stood up abruptly.

The drive home felt a lot quicker than the ride to the restaurant at the beginning of the night. It was just before eleven p.m. when she pulled into her driveway. She turned off the ignition and sat in the quiet, letting all the details of the evening settle in. James had exited The Bistro only steps behind her, practically chasing her across the parking lot. He'd called out her name and she'd stopped. With her back still to him, she took a deep breath and clenched her eyes shut, as if trying to erase everything that had just happened. He approached her from behind and stood quietly for a second before placing his hand on her shoulder and caressing her arm. She panicked. She spun around to face him and went for the most casual scripted exit she could think of. Her options were extreme politeness or complete devastation, and she chose the road less crazy, had told him *how good it was* to see him.

They'd shaken hands like new strangers or old acquaintances; either way, it wasn't natural. He lingered for a moment before she finally pulled her hand out of his and opened her car door to signal that she had to go. Deep down she didn't really want to leave, not like that, but she honestly couldn't bear the disconsolate air between them. She wished she could go back

inside to their quiet, intimate table and tell him everything she
had been holding back; she wanted to tell him that she loved
him and ask if he still loved her. She needed to ask him if he
wanted to be with this other girl. *Lots of people have babies
together who aren't couples,* she'd told herself, picturing actress
Kate Hudson and her ex-rocker with the long hair, whatever
his name was. But she hadn't said any of that to James; she had
just gotten into her car and driven off.

Now, alone in her driveway, she sighed heavily, wishing
so badly she had done things differently. She looked toward
her living room window and noticed the curtains being moved
to the side, Charlie's head pressing against the glass. He knew
she was home and would start barking any second if she didn't
come inside.

She opened the car door using her entire body and stepped
out onto her cracked cement driveway just as a cold gust of
wind came through. She dashed down the sidewalk and onto
the front stoop, flung the glass storm door open, and held it with
her elbow as her hands fumbled with the keys. Stepping into
the foyer a moment later, she was greeted by instant warmth
and Charlie. She briefly petted him between his ears, then
turned back to the door to latch the chain lock and the dead
bolt. Feeling as worn out as if she'd just finished a long run, she
leaned her back against the door and questioned the last five
years of her life. She was alone and could cry or scream if she
wanted to—no one was there to judge her—but she didn't even
have the energy for that. She tossed her keys onto the small
entryway table as she passed through the foyer and continued
to her bedroom. She dropped her purse on the floor next to
her nightstand, where a large bouquet of white tulips stood in a
pale-blue glass vase. She stood still for a moment before falling
backward, collapsing on her neatly made bed, sinking into the
cloudlike white duvet. Charlie sat attentively at the foot of her

bed as if he were keeping an eye on her, then suddenly made a quick exit toward the living room. Corinne pushed herself halfway up onto her elbows and furrowed her brows, listening for a clue as to what her dog was up to, when she heard him whining at the front door. And then there was a knock.

Startled, she sat straight up in her bed, completely alert, and looked around, hoping it was her imagination. Who would be at her door at this time of night? Charlie let out a howl, confirming someone was there. This time Corinne jumped out of the bed and cautiously began to approach the foyer. As she neared the door that was locked up like Fort Knox, she first attempted to see who was on the stoop by subtly moving back the curtain and peeking out of the window, but she was unsuccessful. She hadn't locked the glass door, and it appeared to be open, so whoever it was was standing right there. Before she could react (or overreact), she was able to make out what appeared to be a dark SUV parked on the street. Her stomach fell to the floor and her heart started to beat a little faster, and she quietly unlocked the dead bolt and the chain. Her heart was racing as she reminded herself that it was over, but it didn't feel that way. She creaked the door open a few inches.

James was standing in her doorway with one arm propped against her house as if it were the only thing holding up his entire body; the storm door was pushed all the way open behind him. It smelled like rain outside, and the air was thick and moist. His eyes looked vulnerable, his shoulders appeared tired, and his head was hanging low like he was the most shameful man in the world. She told herself to make him leave, that he needed to be home with the mother of his child, but instead she just stood there quietly and patiently. He lifted his gaze to meet hers, and she saw what looked like pain and maybe even regret in his eyes. She knew that look, because she too felt that same way when it came to him. He shook his head and let out a sigh that sounded like he had been carrying it around for a while. There was something he wanted to say, but the words weren't coming together for him.

It hurt her heart to see him like this, and she started to feel sorry for him. She assumed he needed closure, her forgiveness, to move on with his new family. Corinne knew what she had to do. She had to release him with no hard feelings. She could let him off the hook by simply telling him that everything was okay, and that she had moved on, and that he was doing the right thing by being with this woman. She considered this plan but only for a second. Instead, she took a deep breath and started a speech that would remind him how they met too young and fell in love too soon, convince him that they'd gone in different directions in life . . . but she hesitated when he started to say something at the same time she did.

"I'm sorry, I . . ." He stopped midsentence.

This was the moment they both allowed themselves to feel something that they had been pushing away, like a forbidden fruit, for so long. This was the exact moment when doing the right thing no longer seemed feasible. What seemed like the right thing to do and what Corinne actually wanted to do were two completely different things, and she was tired of talking herself off the edge of a cliff—she wanted to jump. The air was still, her breath was shallow, and his body language spoke volumes. This was the moment they had been waiting for.

He pushed through the doorway and wrapped one arm around her waist. She held on to him, lacing her fingers together behind his neck and standing on her tiptoes. His breath was deep and heavy in her hair, her lips pressed against his neck, as he backed her into the foyer and up against a wall. She pushed him back so she could look him in the eye; he was staring at her, looking her up and down, taking everything in, neither one of them saying anything. His tongue grazed his bottom lip, and she could feel herself melting into him, desiring everything about him. Her insides twisted and her body tingled, like an itch that worsens the more you think about not scratching it. Breathing harder now, her chest was noticeably rising and falling as she slowly started to lean in, her eyes searching his like an unanswered prayer. James seemed almost angry, but not at her. He was angry with himself. He pulled her into him by the waist, gripping her hips, and their lips finally touched for the first time in years. It was soft but severe; the salt on their skin and every caress of their tongues quickened their breaths, pulling them deeper into each other's mouths. Their chemistry was electric, and neither one of them could even think about stopping at this point. Theirs was the kind of passion that didn't have to be worked on or improved. It was intense and rattling; it was raw and relentless. Without missing a beat, he lifted her off the floor, holding on to her thighs. She wrapped her legs around him as he carried her to the bedroom, kicking the door shut behind them.

CHAPTER 13

MY SISTER'S WEDDING

CORINNE

Just over six months had passed since James and I had decided to "take a break," also known as the breakup. It was the first Saturday of March 2012; an insanely crisp and clear afternoon just minutes away from where I grew up in Winston-Salem, North Carolina, and the perfect day for a wedding. Individual knit blankets were draped over each guest's chair, and hot tea and cider were being served prior to the ceremony; outdoor heaters surrounded the big white tent that was laced with patio string lights. It was beautiful, and my sister was completely calm, especially for a bride. Most people might have assumed that, being the control-freak, perfectionist type that she is, she would have been a "bridezilla," but she was on cloud nine, where stress and OCD couldn't touch her. Ava is younger than me by three years—so a pretty young bride, tying the knot at twenty-three—but Ava has always been sure of everything she does. She applied to only one college and attended school there for all four years; she chose a major by the second semester of her freshman year and stuck to it; she dated one guy in high school, Andrew, and stayed with him all through college; after college, he became her fiancé, and today, March 3, he would become her husband. Ava chose March 3 because "it looked like spring but felt like winter"; she liked the idea of possible snow flurries paired with pastels.

Ava looked flawless; her ivory mermaid gown hugged her petite waist and curvy hips, then flared out like a bouquet of flowers at the bottom. She wore her golden hair pulled back into a loose updo with soft curls around her face. Black cat-eye liner and dark mascara made her eyes pop, and she painted her lips a bold, classic red. She looked like a timeless doll in a special-edition box that you weren't allowed to play with or even open.

I was her maid of honor and stood by her side along with a few bridesmaids. First there was her childhood friend Lane, better known as Laney. They met back in middle school before Ava discovered contacts and Laney was still rocking neon-green rubber bands in her braces. They had grown up together and been through everything, including the white eyeliner phase and the tanning bed era. Laney was an art teacher at the same high school we graduated from. The other brides-maid was Andrew's sister, Alison. She was a few years older than Andrew and very outgoing. Heels every day, all day, no matter what the occasion. Her shoulder-length brown hair was always neatly smoothed and flatironed. Laney and Alison wore matching rose-colored floor-length dresses, and their hair was up in traditional buns. As I was the maid of honor, Ava picked out something special for me. It was a soft cream-colored gown, made with vintage lace from the wide, elegant neckline down to the hips; the lower half was the most delicate tulle I had ever seen, and it hung straight down to the floor. The sleeves were capped and hung off my shoulders, made with the same vintage lace as the bodice. She thought it was perfect for the maid of honor role; personally, I felt like I could be the one getting married in a dress like it. However, I was recently single, so marriage wasn't exactly in the cards at the moment.

After our difficult period, James and I had decided to take some time apart to "focus on ourselves." I totally understood the reason for the "break" at the time, but now I couldn't help but think that it wasn't *really* for me, even though it had seemed like it was a mutual decision. James had just graduated from UNCW that May and was focused on finding his niche in the working world. I had no plans of waiting tables forever, but for the time being I was fine with it and pretty good at it. However, about a month after the break, I decided that if James was using this time to better himself, then I was going to do the same. I just had to figure out how.

My first idea of how to better my situation was to get a new job. I had been waiting tables since college graduation in 2008, almost four years. It definitely wouldn't be a bad idea to try my hand out at something new, maybe something I went to school for. Perhaps a job with some health insurance and benefit plans, maybe even some paid vacation time. It was all kinds of exciting to think about. Something else I decided to start doing again in order to focus on myself was writing. I needed to throw myself back into something I was passionate about, something that was just about me and no one else. I'd always had a thing for writing and had often been told I was pretty decent at it. Maybe it was time to start a novel, or a book of poetry; yes, that was exactly what I was going to do.

During the wedding, some of the older guests attempted heartfelt talks, asking me how I felt about my little sister getting married first, and letting me know that there was still time for me, while also reminding me that my biological clock was ticking away. They held my hand and patted me on the shoulder, taking pity on my "circumstance," pity that I did not want and most definitely didn't need. I usually responded with a wink, a raise of a glass of champagne, and a candid comment about feminism. We have a very large family, so you can imagine how drunk I was by the time the wedding cake was cut. I really started to wish my friend Meghan could've made it. A wingman would have come in handy at a time like this.

I totally could have had a date if I'd wanted one. Absolutely. One call to my college flame, Christopher, and he would've been right there by my side. He'd always been there for me, through the ups and downs of the Corinne and James saga. But for some reason, I knew I wasn't quite ready for that kind of distraction yet. Plus, I was pretty sure I had seen on Facebook that he was dating someone, and the last thing I needed was the girl drama that would inevitably follow if he accepted my invitation to the wedding.

While Ava and Andrew were sweetly hand-feeding each other tiny cake bites, I was befriending the bartender, who kept my glass filled with champagne. The DJ played all the wedding classics, such as "The Electric Slide," the "Cupid Shuffle," and the infamous "Macarena." They were a hit with most of the wedding guests; I, however, happily declined to take part in the line-dance craze. I wasn't embarrassed, not one bit actually. I had been drinking all night, so the word "embarrassed" was no longer in my vocabulary. I'm not a line dancer, period. At some point, I became too needy for the bartender, asking him to constantly pour me more wine, so he traded me a bottle of Moët for my empty glass. This led me to an impromptu speech in which I babbled about true love, finding yourself, and some completely unrelated randomness about ships and the ocean,

I don't know; I raised my half-empty bottle and rambled and called it a toast. Luckily, Ava wasn't mad. She knew my drunk and dramatic side better than most and helped me pull myself together, first by taking away the microphone and the champagne and second by force-feeding me a leftover dinner roll and multiple glasses of water.

At the end of the night, everyone stood around holding sparklers as Ava and Andrew prepared for their exit. Not me, though—my sparkler privilege had been revoked, and I was carrying my shoes instead. I was starting to feel a little more clearheaded as I watched them holding hands and running toward their limousine. Still a little unstable, I could feel myself swaying, and I placed one hand on the limo to balance myself, and just before Ava jumped in the car, she leaned over to whisper something in my ear. I'll never forget what she said.

"He didn't even want you, so why would you want him?"

I furrowed my brows, feeling offended or maybe a little dizzy from all of the alcohol. *Such a rude little know-it-all in her fancy wedding dress, like she's the only person any guy can love.* I rolled my eyes, which I thought was pretty subtle, but trust me, nothing I do while under the influence is subtle, and of course she noticed.

"Oh, come on, Corinne. Don't be mad at me. You know I love you, but I know how you work. Do *not* call him tonight. I promise you nothing good will come from that," she said.

And just then her husband swept her into the limo and they drove off. I wasn't sure if I should've felt as lonely as I did right then, but I couldn't help it. Guests began leaving right away. I didn't move for a few minutes as I watched the red taillights burn out into the night. I knew Ava meant well; her advice was meant to be sweet. Deep down I knew she was right, but I truly didn't care. I stumbled back into the reception area to find my phone. My little black clutch was lying underneath a table littered with half-empty beers and wineglasses. On all fours I awkwardly crawled under the floor-length tablecloth and retrieved the miniature purse. The red lipstick seemed too ritzy of a color for my current mood, but I put it on anyway. It made me feel better. I sat cross-legged on the floor, and the first person I called was a cab, because I honestly didn't feel like spending the night at my parents'. The plan was to get a cab to take me to a nearby hotel, get a single room, and sleep until noon the next day.

While waiting for my ride, I went to the bathroom, neglecting to put my shoes back on my feet before doing so. The train of my elegant dress in one hand and my phone in the other, I unsteadily fumbled my way into the tiny first stall, not even bothering to close the door all the way, and slumped down on the closed toilet lid. I thumbed through my contacts until I came to James's name, and my eyes squinted in an effort to correct my blurred vision. I didn't take into consideration that it was after one in the morning and that he may have been asleep or quite possibly out on the town somewhere, perhaps even with a girl; none of those thoughts crossed my mind before I hit "Call."

To my surprise and relief, a very sleepy-sounding James answered the phone after the third ring.

"Corinne, are you okay?" he asked with a hint of genuine concern in his voice.

I definitely didn't call with the intention of alarming him, so I quickly put his mind to ease by reassuring him that I was fine.

"I'm at the wedding of the year, didn't you know? Super dressed up and stuff, you should see it," I said playfully.

"That sounds enticing, be there in ten," he joked.

I laughed and got resituated on the closed throne. "You're funny," I said simply and honestly.

"So you're all good over there? Looking like a dream, no doubt. You got a hot date around?" He tried to sound like he was kidding, but his curiosity was very apparent.

"Nope. I'm stag, my dear." I looked around the bathroom, feeling foolish and suddenly very thankful he couldn't see me. "I'm actually about to head out, maybe grab a drink with some bridesmaids before last call." Completely untrue. "I just wanted to call and say hi real quick."

"Well, I'm really glad you did." There was a long pause. "I've missed you," he said.

I closed my eyes and smiled but also kind of wanted to cry. "I miss you . . . like, all the time," I said, still smiling but trying to steady my voice as I held back the tears.

"Be careful getting home tonight, okay?"

"I will . . ." I assured him. It was quiet for a second, like we were both waiting on the other person to say something else, anything at all, when finally he spoke up.

"I love you, Corinne."

I bit my lower lip and held my left hand to my heart. "I love you too, James." And with that, a single tear ran down my cheek.

CHAPTER 14

THE DISAPPEARING ACT

CORINNE

I sat wide awake and alone, unsure if it was late or perhaps just really early. It was that strange time of day just before the sun rises when the sky is still dark, but hints and shapes of trees and the skyline are beginning to take shape. The stars were still shining in the navy sky while hues of purple and pink began to creep in. The opaque moon was barely visible from the smoky-gray clouds hovering low in the sky. It had started raining at some point after James had shown up. There was no way that I could fall asleep now, so I sat up in my bed, leaning against the upholstered headboard wearing only my bra and underwear, the same ones that I had so carefully picked out earlier that night, my white duvet wrapped around my chest.

I kept thinking back to just a few short hours ago when James was carrying me through my house and into the bedroom, where he'd gently laid me across the bed while making his way on top of me, our lips never parting. I recalled the rain as it began to fall, softly at first, but soon picking up momentum, getting heavier by the minute as if trying to keep up with what was going on in my bed. I never would have guessed we were only minutes away from a phone call that would bring everything to a screeching halt.

Buttons were ripped off his shirt and scattered across the wood floors, our shoes kicked off in different directions, and my shirt wasn't even off before his hands had moved toward the buttons on my jeans. It was crazy to me how long it took for me to get dressed compared to how quickly someone else was able to undress me. I had no complaints at that moment. James could do whatever he wanted with me. His jeans hung low on his hips while he was busy tending to my wardrobe. It was the kind of stuff you read about in romance novels, and it was unfolding in my room.

Then James's phone rang, and this time, I wasn't the one calling him.

Startled by the sound, he shot up toward the foot of the bed, climbing over me, and began frantically digging around in his pocket for his phone. When he saw the name lighting up the screen he instantly said, "Oh God" like he'd forgotten I was in the room, and answered it without wasting another second. Only able to hear one side of the conversation, I was in the dark, but it didn't take me long to uncover what—or should I say *whom*—it was concerning. He said things like "Where is she?" and "Is she okay?" and wrapped up the call with my all-time favorite when he said, "I'll be right there." I felt like I was going to pass out. I think I was subconsciously holding my breath for the duration of the phone call. I guess it was a good thing she wasn't long-winded or anything.

I sat still without saying a word. Honestly, what was I supposed to say? Riddled with embarrassment and guilt, I just
watched him dart around my room in an effort to get his things
and hit the road to get back to her. And who could blame him?
She was having his baby.

It was pretty dumb of me, really, to not have taken a second
to ask or even wonder where his girlfriend was while we were
having dinner, while he was on my doorstep, and, soon after
that, in my bed. I mean, she had to have been wondering where
he was all night. I blame my lapse in judgment on a moment of
pure insanity and bliss.

I felt ashamed and dirty, like "the other woman" kind of
dirty. Even though the phone call had interrupted things
before they could go *too* far, it still made me feel horrible. All
this time I'd felt so disconnected from his real life because I
was constantly reminding myself of *our* history, like his current
state was just a sad and unfair twist in our love story before our
happily ever after. But this wasn't some fairy tale, and these
weren't characters in a book; they were real people. What they
had was more than just a fling; it was more relevant than our
shared past, because it was the present. I had been so sure that
James being with this other woman was the mistake, when in
reality it seemed like the mistake he was making was with me.

I watched his half-naked body move across the room, the
same body that had been lying next to mine, the same body
that had created a life with another woman, and it made my
stomach ache. Just as he was about to leave, he stopped suddenly and leaned over the bed to quickly kiss me good-bye.
With all the commotion and stress, I thought he might've
actually forgotten that I was still sitting there. He kissed my
cheek, his lips soft and warm, and with a heavy sigh whispered,
"I'm sorry." Those words seemed kind of insignificant for the

humiliation of my situation, but honestly, what else could he have said? Let's do this again sometime?

Hurriedly, he turned to leave, and the sleeve of his coat grazed the tall blue vase that sat on my nightstand. It rocked unsteadily for a second before crashing to the ground, scattering white tulips across the floor. He looked back at me one last time, his face ridden with guilt, like he wanted to clean up his mess in more ways than one, but also like he *really* needed to go, like right that second. He paused for only a moment and said, "Please forgive me. Nicole needs me . . ." And just like that he was gone and I was left with the memory and the image of exactly who *she* was.

I buried my face into my hands. I wanted to scream, but I just sat there in silence instead. I could hear Charlie's paws clicking across the wooden floor and entering the bedroom to investigate the crime scene. I didn't move from my fixed position against the headboard until he hopped up on the bed and rested his head on my knees, as if he were truly concerned. Finally, I lifted my head and hugged Charlie, incredibly thankful for his company. Just then I heard some birds chirping outside, taking shelter from the rain up against the house, resting on the windowsill. They looked cold, and I couldn't help but think that if they were still flying south for the winter, how I wished they'd take me with them.

CHAPTER 15

THE WHISKEY

In early September of 2013, roughly one year and one month before the fateful evening when she'd found out James was going to be a father, Corinne ran into him for the final time as a single man. He wasn't even on her mind that night. She was single, too, and living in the moment as she walked through the charming downtown streets of Wilmington. It was much too cool for a late-summer evening, but she wore her lucky little green dress anyway. It was her favorite dress, and not just because the thin, lacy neckline hung off her bare shoulders, or because it hugged her delicate waist, or even because it was short and pleated and fun to twirl in. This dress had been bringing her luck since she first wore it on New Year's Eve in 2009, and she felt she could use that sort of luck tonight. It was the first date Corinne had been on in six months. Making her way down Front Street and over the crosswalk with other nameless pedestrians, she reached a little hole-in-the-wall called The Whiskey where she would be meeting her date. He had offered to pick her up, but she preferred to arrive on her own; that way she could make an easy escape in case the night wasn't going as well as she anticipated.

Standing in the doorway, she flashed a flirtatious smile and her ID to Evan, the bouncer. She had been to enough shows at this bar that he really didn't need to see it, but it was protocol. Besides, with a face like hers, she wasn't easily forgotten, and by the grin on Evan's face, it was clear he remembered her.

Her high heels announced her arrival as she stepped into the bar and examined her surroundings. The band was still setting up, so the jukebox was filling in for the time being. There was a small herd of girls gathered next to the band's crew members; they looked to be twentysomething, so that probably meant that they were eighteen. Corinne scanned the room to her right, but there was still no sign of her date.

Not a problem, she thought. She didn't mind taking a seat at the half-empty bar and grabbing a drink before he arrived. Death Cab for Cutie was playing on the jukebox, which tickled her even more. There was a television playing a baseball game over the bar, but thankfully it was on silent, so it didn't interfere with one of her favorites, "Summer Skin." She sang the words under her breath while getting situated on a wobbly stool, placing her phone and mint-green wristlet on the bar. She hated when the stools wobbled and thought about moving down one when the bartender interrupted her thoughts, laying a coaster down in front of her.

"Oh, I'll have a . . ." she began, pausing as if she were truly contemplating what she would order. She got the usual. "I'll just have a glass of merlot. Thank you."

The bartender nodded and smiled. He, too, remembered Corinne and knew that merlot was her go-to drink. He gave her a very heavy pour and set it on the coaster so efficiently that she was over the idea of swapping barstools. The glass was too full to pick up, so she had to lean over and sip it down a bit first. As she did, the bartender looked at her to assess her reaction to his very generous pour; she winked at him midswallow to show her gratitude, and he gave another nod.

The band had begun running through a sound check; there was some tapping on the microphone, and a speaker let out a screech that caused the growing crowd to cringe in unison. Her glass was half empty when she heard her name.

"Corinne." It wasn't a question but a statement; that voice could only belong to one man. Her eyes widened as she swiveled her entire stool around and smiled, trying not to look too caught off guard.

"James," she said back, genuinely reciprocating his admiration. "I didn't know you were coming to this show." Her voice was coy as she tried to play it cool.

"I didn't know it either, actually—it just kind of . . . came up. I'm not gonna lie, though, I thought I might see you up here"—he paused long enough to smile back—"when I saw The Walkmen were playing tonight."

Why was he so gorgeous without knowing it and so good with words without trying? Everything that came out of his mouth sounded better just because it was him. "I do love them— you remembered." She smiled appreciatively; the thought of him knowing her made her want to melt. He motioned to the bartender, holding up two fingers. Without questioning, the bartender sat two beers on the bar in front of Corinne.

"Oh! I'm actually okay, I've still got a sip or two left," she said as she pointed to her nearly empty glass, "but thank you, seriously." Her stomach fluttered with butterflies at the sight of James standing so close to her and buying her a drink. The night felt anew with purpose, like fate was staging an intervention. She was reconsidering his offer of the drink when she saw a tall brunette approaching him from behind. The woman got closer, and her eyes seemed to be zeroed in on James. When she reached the bar, all suspicions were confirmed as she leaned in toward James and across Corinne's lap for the beer. She smiled and thanked him for the drink. James said nothing but nodded politely and pointed to a corner table with two chairs. She then smiled at Corinne like "nice to meet you but not really because we didn't even meet—okay, bye"—at least that's what it felt like to Corinne. Then she walked off to their table, waiting for James to join her.

James waited until his date had sat down and then tried to explain. "I'm so sorry if that was awkward. I'm actually here with someone tonight—well, her name is Nicole. I'm here with Nicole tonight. I didn't know if I was supposed to mention that to you or not, you know? I just saw you sitting up here by yourself, and we haven't talked in a while so I wanted to—"

Corinne interrupted him. "Me? No, no, I'm not alone; I'm just currently sitting alone. I'm also here with someone tonight." She sat a little taller and looked around the room for her date, who was officially late. "Or I will be. Someone will be meeting me here is what I'm trying to say." She could hear herself rambling; she could feel herself sinking. "I don't even drink beer. Well, I mean, I do, or I would, it's just I like wine. I really prefer red wine." It was quiet. She had *finally* stopped talking.

She could tell he still felt a little embarrassed by her misreading of the situation, but he smiled and shook his head.

"Corinne, you're still the most beautiful and intriguing woman I've ever met. It was really good running into you." He sounded like he meant what he said, and his eyes confirmed it. He started to turn to walk over to Nicole when he stopped suddenly and looked Corinne up and down one last time. His expression was precise and coercive. "That dress, though . . ." He walked away and she broke into a million pieces, but only on the inside.

Moments later, the band was roaring and Corinne's date had finally arrived, running to her side like he was rushing to the scene of an emergency. He had to shout over the music to explain to her all about his crazy day at work and a deadline for a big project he was overseeing and how his cat was scheduled to be declawed later that week. The whole time, she kept one hand on the hem of her dress, running her fingers across the lace; the other hand clutched a fresh pour of wine as if it were a lifeline. *Who is this Nicole girl anyway?* She was pretty, that was for certain. But even though Corinne was very jealous at the sight of them together, she told herself that the chances of them actually ending up together were very slim. At this point, all she wanted to do was listen to the band and polish off an entire bottle, and this poor guy sitting next to her was clueless—clueless that this would be their one and only date and that he was undoubtedly going home alone tonight. Regardless, this was her favorite dress, and she was glad she had worn it.

CHAPTER 16

WESTBOUND HOME

Less than twenty-four hours had passed since the passionate almost sex with James, and it was consuming her mind. She was heading down Interstate 40 westbound toward her hometown, and the drive allotted her more time to think than she had wanted. The images from that night were haunting her, but the truth was something else had been bothering her too— some*one* else, more specifically. She hadn't seen her mom in over a month, and when she would allow herself to truly think about it, she was racked with guilt. It was time to face the music, in multiple areas of her life, and she knew without a doubt that it was time to go home for a while.

Shortly after James's disappearing act, Corinne had managed to pull herself together for the sake of her job. She had more than enough time to get ready for work, so she moved slowly, beginning with a cold shower. Her eyes felt swollen; the cool water relieved some of the puffiness. A large part of her was insanely sad to wash away his scent that stayed behind in her hair and on her skin. But she was also riddled with guilt, so she decided to use half a bottle of her vanilla-orange-scented shampoo to do the trick. Taking a clean stone-gray wash-cloth, she lathered it with soap and began scrubbing her entire body, starting with her face. Remnants of lingering mascara smeared lightly along the corner of the cloth. She worked her way down her thin, tired body, feeling restless and fatigued from the motion, and then took a seat on the shower floor as she scrubbed her feet. She was covered in chill bumps from the cool water and shivered as it continued to run freely over her, but she had no desire to turn it off. In a weird way, it felt good to feel discomfort, almost like she was punishing herself for her thoughts and, even worse, her actions. Finally, without standing, she lifted her arm high enough to reach the faucet and turn it off. She instantly felt relief rush over her when the water stopped. But even though she was technically clean, she couldn't shake a certain lingering dirty feeling.

After getting dressed, she started the coffee—stronger than usual, since she hadn't slept. While it was brewing, she sat on the kitchen floor and paid Charlie some much-deserved attention. He put all his weight on Corinne's lap and rolled over for a belly rub. She let out a small laugh, realizing how weak she felt, and wondered what in the hell she would do without that dog. She leaned over and kissed his wet nose while she scratched his belly once more. Checking the time on the microwave clock, she thought about calling her mom. Despite her sickness, she was still an early riser. But Corinne decided not to call; her mom had bigger things to worry about than her daughter's love life.

She stood reluctantly, stretching her arms and fingers straight over her head, allowing blood and oxygen to circulate through her sleep-deprived body. She wouldn't say that she felt good, by any means, but she was at least feeling up to leaving the house for work. Charlie was patiently waiting in the foyer next to where his leash hung, so she opened the door for him, letting him out into the yard. While he was doing his thing, she twisted her long, wavy hair into a loose bun and made one last quick stop in the kitchen. She filled up a large to-go tumbler full of coffee; her stomach was on edge, so she skipped the cream this time. In the foyer, she decided a pretty heavy coat would be necessary for today, so she went for a hunter-green wool pea-coat and added a long royal-blue scarf to complete the look. She heard Charlie's paw scratch against the door and pushed it open just enough for him to slip inside before she turned to leave. She stepped outside into the frigid air and instantly drew her arms tightly into her sides; it was so cold her whole body was contracting on its own. She locked up the house and made a quick dash to her car. She started it up and sat still for a second, hoping to thaw everything out, herself included; her mind went to James and his soft lips and dark eyes, and she immediately felt sick again. She knew she should be glad that things had stopped so suddenly, that the phone call had come when it had, but a small part of her wasn't. She had imagined what it would be like to be with him again for so long, and now it was tainted. Deep down she knew she would've hated herself if they'd actually had sex. There was no good ending to this scenario; it was a catch-22.

She closed her eyes as if to cleanse her mind of those images and thought about her mom again. She missed her and she needed her, more than ever right now. Her mom always said the right things and gave the best advice. "I need to go home," Corinne announced out loud. But she had somewhere else to go at the moment, unfortunately. Completely drained, she pulled out of her driveway and headed to work.

When she arrived at the small dental practice where she had been working for almost two years now, she clocked in and went straight to her desk to turn on her computer. She was the first one there, which almost never happened. She turned on the waiting room lamps and unlocked the front door just as her coworkers began to arrive. She was getting the community coffeepot brewing when she heard her boss walk in through the back door. After pushing the "Brew" button, she went straight to his office.

Mark was a good guy and a good dentist, and a little socially awkward, probably because of how smart he was. Corinne loved the importance he placed on families. He was a family man himself and was very tolerant of the unexpected inconveniences that came with it. His office door was partially open, so Corinne knocked lightly on the doorframe to get his attention. He had just set down his briefcase and was peeling off his wool coat. He looked up at Corinne and smiled, inviting her in.

"Good morning. The coffee should be ready in just a few minutes," she said brightly.

"Okay, that sounds great. Thanks, Corinne." As he directed his attention back to his briefcase, she hesitated, and he looked back at her. "Anything else going on this morning?"

The answer was yes, on many levels. The stress of the last four years—her mother's illness and everything with James, combined with life's other difficulties—felt like it was all hitting her at this one moment. Mark maintained eye contact with her, now with a slight worried look attached. Corinne knew she needed to say something; anything at this point would be better than this stunned deer expression. She could've easily said that she really missed her mom, and also that the love of her life had just walked out on her, and that she felt as tiny and insignificant as a person could feel. She took a deep breath and started to ask about taking a few days off for a chance to go home, but that's not what came out. Her eyes welled up with tears and her face felt red with embarrassment, and instead of speaking, she began to cry.

Mark was a nice guy, but this was definitely out of his comfort zone. He stood with his eyes wide, unsure of what he was supposed to do next, and then he offered her a tissue. With mascara running down her cheeks, and trying to catch her breath between sobs, she accepted the gesture and blew her nose. Instead of asking questions, he urged her to take the next few days off.

Corinne didn't go into detail or say much of anything else besides thanking him for being such a supportive boss. She quickly grabbed her things and left out the back door without saying anything to her other coworkers; there was too much to say, and she didn't know where she would even begin.

It took Charlie by complete surprise when she walked in the front door. He hopped off the couch and raised his butt in a big stretch before he happily met her in the foyer. It wouldn't take her long to pack a bag; she knew she wouldn't need much this entire upcoming weekend at home. She made a mental list: underwear, wool socks, boots, two sweaters, a pair of fleece-lined leggings, one pair of jeans, and a matching flannel pajama set (it was cozy and made her feel good). The basic and necessary toiletries were a given. And Charlie, of course.

After quickly packing, she got both Charlie and herself settled in her still-warm VW. She started the car and buckled up, but before putting the car into drive she dug through a stack of old CDs in her glove compartment. She came across a CD that had crooked, sloppy handwriting in permanent marker written across it. The handwriting was hers and it read, "Go places, write books." She inserted the CD and hoped it wouldn't bring her to tears, which seemed likely. Turning left out of her driveway, she headed for the highway, beyond ready to get out of Wilmington for the next few days. As she waited at a stoplight, she hesitated but decided to quickly check her phone one last time before getting on Interstate 40 for any missed calls or perhaps a text message. There was nothing, really, just an e-mail from a local yoga studio inquiring where she had been for the past few months and asking if she had plans to rejoin. She deleted the e-mail and set her phone back in the cup holder and pressed "Play" on the CD player. The first song on the burned album began to play.

Just before the light turned green, she glanced in the rearview mirror and noticed Charlie was already peacefully snoozing in the backseat. Leaving town was absolutely necessary; there was no doubt about it.

CHAPTER 17

THE ALMOST END

Just before Corinne and James ended their relationship, things had definitely changed. The two couldn't seem to get on the same page, and it had started to get uncomfortable for everyone around them. One night in particular marked the virtual end of them—the kind of night you don't come back from easily.

Blue Post was their favorite spot downtown. It was a small and cozy joint that served beer only, so that alone kept most of the typical college clubbers at bay. A few neon beer signs lit up the band-flyer-covered walls, and the bar's list of craft beers was to be admired by any hipster or brooding, mysterious bass player. That particular night, Corinne and her friend Meghan had worked a shift at the restaurant together before going over to Blue Post to meet James and two of his good buddies. Even though Corinne and Meghan were both UNCW graduates, they hadn't met until they'd started working together at the restaurant. They'd hit it off immediately. They shared the same taste in music and a love for sushi, and they had the same crude sense of humor and bubbly disposition.

The two girls were currently sitting on a couch together, near the pool table. They had been at Blue Post for a while, long enough to play a few rounds of pool and have a few drinks. Now they were taking selfies while waiting for James to bring Corinne another beer.

Almost fifteen minutes later and still no sign of James or a beer, Corinne and Meghan decided to make a trip to the bathroom. They held on to each other, walking arm in arm for stability. When they rounded the corner heading to the bathrooms, they saw James sitting at the bar, taking a swig of a bottle, with another beer—Corinne's, obviously—resting on the bar in front of him. Next to him sat a very busty blonde with a sleeve tattoo, who was also having a drink. The two were talking and laughing. The aspiring Playboy bunny playfully touched his arm while leaning in toward him, projecting her cleavage in an upward and outward motion. True, this would have annoyed Corinne on any day, but tonight she had been drinking and was more than a little pissed off. Meghan grabbed Corinne's hand and tried to pull her toward the bathroom, but after weeks of holding back, Corinne didn't have it in her to let it go tonight.

She barged in on the conversation by placing herself between them, snatched her beer off the bar, and took a swig. When she asked James for an introduction to his "friend," he sighed heavily and rolled his eyes. The busty tattooed girl didn't seem to care much about who Corinne was and introduced herself with a certain cockiness. She was his ex, one of the many. Corinne felt sick; she just wasn't sure if it was the alcohol or the jealousy. Why was he distancing himself from her? Why did his heart seem so restless? She was sad but wanted to be mad. On second thought, she wanted to be home.

James tried to defuse the situation by handing his beer to Corinne and telling her he would be right over after closing out his tab. His ex looked amused by James's suggestion and smiled at Corinne. Her smugness was infuriating, but what was even worse was the fact that he was trying to pacify Corinne with a drink. Suddenly, she felt dumb and insignificant instead of sad or angry. She shoved his beer back at him and downed the rest of hers right in front of them, then she proceeded to the bar's exit. Refusing Meghan's offer of a ride, she walked the whole way to James's downtown apartment. James arrived home shortly after she did, and he was braced for a fight.

Because of the alcohol, nothing was making sense to either of them and nothing was being resolved, but because of the recent turmoil in the relationship and the lack of apologies, everything was spiraling out of control. He immediately cornered her in the kitchen where she had already begun to pour a glass of wine. James snatched the bottle from her hand and began to empty the rest down the sink. She shoved past him with the glass in her hand, but before she could take another step, he swiped the half-full drink from her and smashed it into the sink, sending a shower of red wine and shards of glass across the white linoleum floor. In retaliation, Corinne marched furiously through the living room where James kept a small record player and an impressive collection of new and vintage records. She tore every album from the shelf and began throwing them out of the cracked window of his second-story apartment. After a moment of shock, James grabbed her by the wrists and yelled at the top of his lungs, "Jesus Christ, Corinne! What the fuck are we even *doing*?"

She had never really heard him raise his voice before. It was weird and scary; they had become totally unrecognizable at this moment. A sobering and ill feeling came over Corinne as she looked around the room. James released her wrists, looking just as disturbed as she was.

Without saying a word, he left the apartment to recover his album collection. Corinne wiped her eyes and walked back into the kitchen, where she grabbed a towel and dropped to her knees. She cleaned as much of the mess as she could and went straight to bed, without James. At some point in the night she heard him come back inside but he never made his way to the bedroom. Everything between them felt like it had gone dead. So much was happening, yet nothing had really happened at all. The next morning was a bit of an awkward mess, emotionally and in the apartment. The day started out slow as they each nursed a lingering headache. Too embarrassed to discuss what had happened, they quietly cleaned up their mess while trying to avoid eye contact. It was as if they both agreed that they should focus on one disaster at a time. When the apartment was put back in order they had to face each other. He started it off by apologizing, but before he could even specify what for, she was already conceding.

The funny thing about guilt is that it clouds your otherwise good judgment. It had become hard for them to see past the turmoil they were creating. Their relationship was fading, but instead of healthily coming to terms with that, they were unknowingly destroying each other on the way out. On this particular day, those thoughts were pushed deep down to a place where they couldn't harm or disappoint anyone. They spent the day together cuddled on the couch watching movies and cooking dinner. Although it resembled a good day on the surface, they both knew the end was near.

CHAPTER 18

THE BREAKUP

The day that James and Corinne decided to call it quits was one of the hottest days of the summer in 2011. There was a heat advisory for that whole week, and the August air was smothering and relentless. This day in particular seemed heavy and dead; the air was completely still. Even the seagulls had taken cover under the Johnnie Mercer's pier instead of scouring the beaches for chips and sandwiches left behind by tourists.

Corinne was just beginning to wake up early that Sunday morning, but before opening her eyes, she stretched out her arm to feel around on his side of the bed, only to find herself alone. James's small, loft-style downtown apartment was extremely hot, and the thin cotton sheets were sticking to her legs as she sat up to look around the upstairs. James was not there; Charlie was, however. For a second she was confused, momentarily forgetting that she had decided to bring him with her the night before in case they decided to stay at James's.

She checked the digital clock on the nightstand: 7:10 a.m. Even after a late night out, she still couldn't make herself sleep in. Just then she heard the rattling and clanking of dishes and running water in the kitchen below her. Giving her temples a gentle massage, she realized she was on the verge of an alcohol-induced headache, so she moved carefully as she peeled the soft gray sheets off her skin and swung her legs around to the side of the bed. Wearing only her underwear and one of James's old T-shirts with an obscure band logo faded across the front, she slipped into the small half bath connected to the bedroom and quietly closed the door. She splashed cold water on her face and brushed her teeth; while examining herself in the mirror, she wondered what James's frame of mind might be this morning. She had a feeling he might still be moody toward her from the previous night and dreaded that conversation if so.

She remembered back to the ride home from the bar; Dave, a coworker, had offered to give her a lift back to James's place, since he hadn't made it out to the bars that night. She and Dave were friendly work acquaintances, but she had heard things about him from other coworkers, rumors about his pushy and dominating behavior with women, especially while drinking. Still, Corinne didn't feel like she would ever be targeted by him for a few reasons: she had a boyfriend that everyone knew about, and also because "no one would ever do such a thing to someone like her." She was the sweet one that everyone liked and looked out for, like a little sister. But while Dave was dropping her off, his good deed had turned into an unwanted advance—he made a move on her.

She replayed the scene in her head again while pressing a cold rag over her puffy eyes; she remembered him pulling up to the curb outside of James's apartment and placing his hand on her thigh. Even though she had been drinking, she was far from drunk and knew exactly what was going on as she shoved his hand off her leg, then immediately reached for the car door to make it clear that nothing was about to happen between them. That's when he grabbed her arm, pulling her into the car, causing her to fall back into the passenger seat. He quickly leaned far across the car console, practically on top of her. Corinne slapped him across his face and yelled, "What the hell!" She kicked his car door wide open and slammed it shut behind her. She hadn't told James about it when she got upstairs to the apartment, one, because she was too tired to rehash the borderline assault and, two, because James would seriously have killed him, like drive over to his house, drag him out of his bed, and literally kill him. But now it was the morning after, and she knew she had to be honest with him. The thought of telling him wouldn't have been so bad if they hadn't already gotten in a fight earlier that night, before she left to go to the bar without him.

She opened the medicine cabinet above the sink and took out some eyedrops and ChapStick. Her eyes clearer and lips moisturized, she finally left the bathroom feeling a tiny bit more human, and slowly crept down the wooden staircase.

The night before was supposed to have been a good one. Some of Corinne's coworkers were going downtown after work. She had the night off, so she had brought Charlie over to James's apartment earlier that evening, before the two of them went out to dinner. The night started out fine, a low-key dinner at their favorite sushi place and a walk down by the Cape Fear River while their food settled. Though it had all begun okay, something definitely seemed off; the conversation felt superficial and rehearsed, and James wouldn't put his phone down for more than five minutes at a time. Instead of attempting to revive the conversation, Corinne trolled her social media out-lets and posted pictures of sushi. By the time they got back to his place, she was more than ready to go out with some friends and have a few drinks.

James put Charlie on his leash and took him downstairs for a short walk to stretch his legs; meanwhile, Corinne dashed up the stairs, changed into her four-inch suede heels, and applied a fresh coat of lip gloss as well as a spritz of her favorite per-fume. She was standing in the kitchen smelling an opened bot-tle of wine to assess its freshness when James walked through the door, letting Charlie off the leash. He continued to stand there for a second watching Corinne taste test the wine. She made a face and poured the remaining cabernet down the drain. James walked the few steps to the living room, kicked off his shoes, and plopped down on the couch next to the sleep-ing pup. He looked comfortable. Too comfortable. Before she could ask if he was ready, he informed her that he would not be going out, but that he didn't care if she still went. It took less than a minute to turn into a full-fledged argument in which she said he had changed and accused him of being boring. Other aspects of the argument included James's observation that a majority of her coworkers were "a bunch of creepy pervs." She took it upon herself to end the conversation and decided to go out anyway.

Now, she reached the last step and rounded the staircase, which looked directly into the kitchen. She knew James saw her out of his peripheral vision, but he didn't look over at her. She walked farther into the kitchen until she was standing right next to him and hopped up onto the countertop next to the sink where he was washing a whiskey glass from the night before and a cereal bowl from that morning. He finally stopped midrinse and looked at her.

"Hi," she said softly.

"Glad to see you made it home okay last night," he responded, without acknowledging her initial greeting.

"Of course I did." As if she would've gone anywhere else!

"Did you have a good time?" He continued to wash and rinse his cereal spoon.

"Yeah, it was pretty fun. A bunch of people from work were there; that new hostess came and, of course, Meghan was there. It was so funny, she and I actually ordered this bottle of wine and—"

"How did you get home?" he interrupted.

She was quiet for a moment and for a split second considered not telling the truth, but she knew she didn't have it in her to lie to him. She paused and slightly bit her lower lip out of nervousness while he laid all the clean dishes on a towel to dry. He looked at her, waiting for a reply.

"Dave gave me a ride."

"Oh great, that was *really* nice of Dave," he said, with no attempt to hide his sarcasm. "Such a good guy, always bending over backward for you in hopes that you'll return the favor . . . literally." His words were crude and etched in disgust. James didn't like Dave, and he definitely did not trust him, and for good reason.

She turned her gaze to the cheap linoleum. "He kind of came on to me." Her eyes stayed glued to the floor, but she could feel his eyes burning into her.

"I'm sorry, what the hell did you just say?"

"When he was dropping me off I was about to get out of the car and he pulled me back like, I don't know, like he was trying to kiss me or something . . ." It sounded as if her thoughts had stopped midsentence, but really she just didn't want to go on.

"Kiss you *or something*?" he shouted. His hands gripped the edge of the sink, and his voice trembled.

"I don't know, I don't know what he wanted to do; he just pulled me back into the car, but I hit him, and that's it, nothing happened!" she shrieked as she began to cry.

"You don't listen to me! You never listen to me about these people! Who do you think cares more about you, me or them? You're like a child sometimes! I swear, Corinne, sometimes I seriously don't even know about . . ." He also stopped midsentence, either to figure out the rest of his thoughts or to keep from saying something he might regret.

"You don't know about what? About me?" she cried, holding her hand against her chest, starting to feel weak and desperate.

"I don't know, Corinne. I honestly don't know what I feel right now." His voice had quieted, and now he seemed more somber than angry. "I just think we're at two different places right now. You're wanting to do one thing and I'm doing another. I'm working on my career and my future, and I don't even know what your plans are." He looked down at the empty sink as if collecting himself, then looked directly into her eyes. "I don't think our paths are going in the same direction . . . at least for now they're not."

She sat in complete silence, feeling stunned. Her body tingled but felt numb at the same time. She could feel her heart in her throat beating so hard she thought she might choke.

"I just . . . I mean I don't . . . What does that mean, exactly?" she finally forced out, dreading the answer.

"I love you, Corinne, I really do." There was a long pause. "I love you . . . but I think it would be best . . . for both of us, if we took some time apart."

She felt like she'd turned to stone, like a gargoyle, doomed to be motionless and alone for all eternity. Feeling faint, she squeezed the edge of the countertop. She knew things had been pretty bad between them, but she still could never imagine him letting her go. While their relationship was turning futile, she'd often wondered if they could ever get to that point where he was just done. Now she no longer had to wonder what that would look or feel like. Here it was.

CHAPTER 19

A REFUGE

CORINNE

It was just after noon when I pulled into my parents' drive-way, announcing to Charlie, "We made it!" He was already well aware of our location, and had been standing in the backseat whining and wagging his tail ever since we'd pulled into their neighborhood. Everything looked the same from the outside. The curtains were neatly pulled back from the windows, a bur-lap wreath hung on the door, the leaves had even been blown out of the flower beds . . . but that didn't fool me. I knew that behind the decorated front door, beyond their well-manicured lawn, was a whole different story.

I suddenly felt like I should've called on the drive down to give them a heads-up. It felt weird thinking that way about my own parents, but these days I never knew what was going on with them on a day-to-day basis. Things can change so quickly, between treatments and just trying to keep up with daily chores and responsibilities. Half of me felt like a burden, and the other half felt like I had abandoned them; it was conflicting and twisted, but I could never shake either one of those notions. I left my weekender bag in the backseat but opened the door for Charlie. The closer I got to the door, the harder I prayed that my mom was having a good day. I wanted to see her smiling. I wanted to hear her laughing. And, most of all, I selfishly wanted her advice and guidance; no, I *needed* her advice and guidance. I climbed the four stairs that led to the covered porch and debated whether I should knock first or just walk in. This was my house, the one I spent thirteen years in before going away to college, so why did I feel like a stranger?

Before I could come to a decision, I heard a rustling coming from inside. The knob creaked and the door swung wide open, Dad standing in the doorway. He was wearing a T-shirt and jeans, looking very casual but very put together. He was strong . . . stable—definitely not the type to break down in front of anyone—so the fact that he looked good didn't really mean that things *were* good; I just liked to assume that it did. He smiled, crinkling the corners of his eyes and showing his age a little, and grabbed me, giving me a huge bear hug; he patted my back and said, "Good to see ya, baby girl." And he meant it, that part I could tell was real for sure. "And you too, Charlie." He leaned over and scratched his ears as Charlie excitedly licked my dad's forearm as his form of *hello*.

"Hey, Dad. How have y'all been?"

"We're doin' all right, sweetie. We've missed you, though. You doing okay?" he said, sounding a tad concerned over my showing up unannounced. Why was he sounding concerned? I should be the one concerned! I hated when he did that, asked a simple question knowing there was more to it than the obvious, always striking a chord with me and usually leading to a breakthrough or a breakdown, either way. It was subtle, but it was invariably accurate. He had a gift for seeing straight through people, even within the first few minutes of meeting them. I often attempted to come across strong and put together, even on a bad day, but he could always see through it. When I was younger, my problems usually consisted of a bad test grade or a fight with a friend, and he always knew how to assure me that he was listening without ever pressuring me to talk. Although today, it made me feel especially guilty because they had bigger problems to deal with other than my love life, if you could even call it that.

"I've missed you guys so much. And yes, Dad, I'm okay," I said as I stepped back from our embrace and smiled reassuringly at him.

"That's all I need to hear." He smiled back at me. "Your mother's going to be happy to see you, that's for sure. Come on in." He wrapped his arm around my shoulders, giving me a gentle squeeze as he and Charlie led me through the entryway into my old home.

I walked slowly through the foyer into the living room, taking notice of every detail: a stack of mail piled up on the kitchen island, a shallow basket full of about thirty different prescription bottles, and two wicker baskets of dirty laundry lined up outside of the laundry room door, waiting to be done. My heart was heavy with guilt. It definitely looked like they could use an extra set of hands, whether they would admit it or not. I made a mental to-do list for the next few days. The staircase was located toward the back of the house, past the kitchen, which was the exact direction we were headed. Charlie made himself comfortable on the cool kitchen tile, and I followed my dad up the stairs at a much slower pace than I'm sure he was used to. With each step I took, I began feeling more anxious. At the top of the stairs, I looked immediately to my left to my room, but that wasn't where we were going. Turning right, I saw my parents' bedroom door was open. The sun was casting a warm golden ray across the dark wooden planks just in front of the door. My dad was no longer leading me; he was right next to me as we walked toward the bedroom. Stopping just outside the door, he put his hand on my shoulder to get my attention.

"You know what, sweetie? I'm going to go downstairs and take Charlie outside for a bit to stretch his legs. I'll get some fresh water for him too."

He smiled and patted my back before turning and briskly jogging back down the stairs. I had no doubts his attentiveness to Charlie's needs was genuine, but I knew he also wanted to give me some time alone with my mom. I stood in front of her bedroom door, feeling the warmth of the sun shining on my legs and feet, took a deep breath, and crossed over the doorway, fully immersing myself into the sunlit room. The master bedroom was huge, with a vaulted ceiling and an entire wall of windows. My mom was sitting up in her bed with her reading glasses on and a book across her lap. Her thin blonde curls were pinned up loosely, and her sweater seemed to swallow her tiny body. She was underneath a thick beige comforter with pillows propped behind her back and neck; besides her weight and hair loss, she looked very much like herself, which was a relief—even if it were misleading. She leaned her head down slightly to look beyond her glasses and said, "Well, this is a surprise!" with a huge smile breaking across her face. I couldn't help but smile back, momentarily forgetting how unfair life was and feeling truly happy.

"Hey, Mom," I said, still standing near her bedroom door.

"Come here! I've missed you!"

I walked over to the bed and hopped onto the edge next to her, like a kid. She closed her book and placed it on her bedside table and held her arms open. She wrapped both arms around me, and we sat there hugging for the next few minutes. I didn't want her to let go, mainly because I didn't want to cry. I started thinking back to when I was a little girl and everything seemed so easy, when I was convinced that rainy days and pop quizzes were as bad as it gets. Being home reminded me of those days. It didn't take long before James popped back into my head, which also made me want to cry. I so badly wanted to talk to her about it; I needed her calming words of wisdom. But it felt much too insignificant to bring up at the moment. I tried to fight back the tears, but the harder I tried, the more they seemed to want to fall.

"Corinne?" she said, sensing something.

As soon as she said it, the river of tears began to flow, and I couldn't even pinpoint the main reason. Suddenly, I realized that the problem was actually a hundred different things. My mother and best friend had cancer. Even though her treatments were going well and the doctor's latest report was a good one, she felt like hell most days. She was tired, beat down, eaten away by the cancer, poisoned by the chemo, and it wasn't fair. On top of that, my job was going nowhere. I was twenty-eight, and my whole dream of a writing career by the time I was thirty was literally all but over. I felt guilty for settling and slightly ridiculous for taking this long to admit it to myself. And then, of course, there was James. I guess a big part of me kept thinking that when we got back together, then life would *really* begin. Never did it actually occur to me to ask, "What if we don't?"

Before I could say anything at all, she said, "You know it's not over for you, don't you?"

It was a strange comment, one I wasn't expecting to hear. My tears slowed and my sobs quieted as I sat up to finally make eye contact. She must have sensed my confusion because she laughed.

"I know how you are, mostly because I'm that way myself." Her smile relaxed me. "Whatever is going on right now in your life, it's not too late to make it how you want it. Make a change, start over, and do it again and again until you're satisfied."

"And what if I have no idea where to begin? What if I don't know what to change first?" I sniffled, feeling seventeen again.

She caught a stray tear running down my cheek with her thumb and wiped it away. "That's the beauty of it. There isn't a right or wrong place to start, there's only doing something or doing absolutely nothing. And you've never been a girl to do nothing . . . so what is it that you want? Happiness, freedom, love? Or do you want it all?"

I knew I wanted it all. She knew I wanted it all. So I said nothing.

"All of those things are very possible to have, Corinne, and they don't all have to come from a single source. Whatever you've been picturing or dreaming of, believing that this solitary idea alone would make all your dreams come true, just erase all that. Don't depend on something or someone to get you what you want."

I suddenly felt like the problems with my love life were unimportant—bigger things were happening here. My eyes were being opened up to ideas and thoughts that sadly hadn't crossed my mind in a very long time. Despite her weak appearance, my mother sounded so strong and confident that it started to make me feel strong and confident. I was tired of crying. I was tired of overthinking. And most of all, I was tired of not doing a damn thing about any of it.

"What is it that *you* want, sweetie?"

I thought hard about the last five years of my life. I thought about that wintry morning at the coffee shop and my first date with James; our carefree days on the beach, when I felt invincible; the shock and fear after finding out my mom had cancer;

my devastation over the breakup. It had felt like the end of everything, when really it was just the end of something—something wonderful, but perhaps something not meant to last. Since then, I had basically put my life on hold, waiting for a moment, an experience, or a person to come and change it all, when the whole time it'd been my story to write. Finally, I thought back to high school and the journal I kept when I first started writing. I needed to read it.

"I just want to be the woman I always imagined I would be," I said quietly.

"You are her. You are her and so much more." She was looking at me very seriously at this point. "You still have no idea what you're capable of. It's inside of you. Find it, feed it, and let it grow furiously."

Cancer had taken a lot of things away from her, but it hadn't touched the fire in her eyes. She kissed my cheek and insisted I get my things and get settled in. Before leaving her room, I took her hand and held it in mine. I wanted to thank her but the words "thank you" didn't seem like enough. The truth is, my parents are amazing people and I could never thank them enough in my entire lifetime. I didn't have to say anything because she already knew . . . She smiled and squeezed my hand before releasing me.

I slid off the side of her bed and left her room, then walked down the hall until I reached a door near the top of the staircase. I turned the bronze doorknob and creaked the door open just wide enough to step in. I hadn't been in my room in a long time; even when I visited home, I usually stayed at my sister's with her and her husband. It looked the same, still painted a pale-mint-green color, still had the same peach quilt on the bed, still had my old white painted antique vanity with an upholstered chair sitting against the wall next to the large window that overlooked the backyard. Ironically, on my old vanity sat a clear vase filled with silk fuchsia tulips. In a strange way, it felt like a sign, just not in the way I would've assumed it meant before.

I pulled open the center drawer in the vanity and found only an old brush. I checked the left drawer next and came across neon-colored nail polishes and a cheap floral perfume. Finally, I opened the right drawer and found a handful of mechanical pencils and my old journal. I glanced out the window into the backyard and saw my dad sitting on the deck with Charlie at his feet. It was a sunny afternoon, and they both seemed to be enjoying the fresh air, so I decided to steal away a little more time to myself and took the journal and hopped onto the center of my bed, still kind of feeling seventeen and loving every second of it.

One hundred and fifteen pages of handwritten journal entries later, I felt inspired, like the younger, untainted me was a motivational speaker and the current me, her audience. I was well aware that it was completely healthy and natural for people to change, and, yes, eleven years later I wouldn't be the same girl I was back then. But that wasn't the point. I just needed a reminder of what it had felt like to be fearless and to believe that anything could happen. I needed to be reminded that once upon a time I was someone who believed in dreams coming true. Once upon a time I was my own hero and my happiness was up to me. The beautiful thing was I finally believed that again, with all of my heart.

I walked back over to the vanity with my journal in hand, grabbed a pencil out of the drawer, and pulled the matching vintage chair out far enough to get seated comfortably. Unsure of what would come out, I started to write. Each sentence that I finished flowed into the next. I couldn't believe I had so much to say. I wrote until my fingers were cramped and my eyes could hardly stay open. It was dark outside when I put my journal and pencil back into the drawer. Charlie had made his way up to my bedroom at some point and was lying just outside of my partially opened bedroom door. I heard him shake as he stood up and nudged the door all the way open with his nose. I pushed the chair back under the vanity and collapsed onto my bed. Charlie followed, curling up right at my feet.

The house was quiet, my stomach was growling, and my fingers felt numb. Overall, I was feeling pretty content. Clasping my hands together over my stomach, I lay comfortably on my childhood bed, stared at the ceiling, and took a deep breath. As I exhaled, I felt a wave of relief rush over me; maybe it was the hours of writing and finally expressing myself so thoroughly again, but one thing was apparent: a huge part of me was excited to wake up the next morning and continue my narrative. At first, I hadn't been sure what I would write about, but once I'd gotten started it was like I just knew.

CHAPTER 20

BITTERSWEET

JAMES

My son was born early Thursday morning, at 5:11 a.m. Nicole was in labor for about five hours, and the delivery itself went pretty smooth, I guess. Not that I have a ton of experience with these kinds of situations. She woke up soon after going to bed Wednesday night with sharp pains in her stomach. They turned out to be contractions. They were getting stronger and closer together way faster than she thought they would, so her sister and mother immediately made the regularly an-hour-and-a-half drive to the hospital in Wilmington in less than an hour. That was where our doctor was, and that was where we had planned on giving birth. Obviously, I made it there before they did and was waiting with Nicole's hospital bag. I paced back and forth, staring at my phone every two seconds, debating whether to call or not, debating *whom* to call. When they finally pulled up to the sliding glass entrance, I was still shaking. My own guilt was playing tricks on my mind and making me paranoid. I swore her sister kept looking at me funny, but I tried to play it cool. Immediately, I helped Nicole into the wheelchair I had brought out to the drop-off area. As I lowered her into the chair, she whispered in my ear, "God, I'm so glad to see you." And she really meant it. I wheeled her through the giant sliding glass doors while her mother and sister went to park the car.

After getting checked in around two a.m. we sat in triage for what seemed like forever. The nurse helped Nicole get undressed and into a hospital gown in between excruciating contractions. Every five minutes, she was bent over moaning in pain until they got her into a bed and hooked up to monitors: one to watch her heart rate and the other to watch the baby's. After that, we were moved into a delivery room where she finally got an epidural. Although I wasn't excited about this part at all, I was just ready for her to finally have some relief. Her brown eyes were filled with tears, but she did her best to hold them back. It was hard to see her in so much pain. I stood off to the side, next to the window, while the anesthesiologist administered the epidural. Less than three minutes later, her whole body had relaxed and she had drifted to sleep. The doctor stopped in to check on her but said there was no rush and we might have to wait a while, since her cervix was only dilated two centimeters. Apparently, you have to be measuring ten to be able to start the pushing part of delivery.

I sat in the chair next to the window, watching the steady rainfall, while Nicole slept just a few feet away from me. Crazy thoughts of texting or even calling Corinne kept entering my mind, and then I would push them away. I felt horrible for not calling her, but I felt even worse for actually wanting to call her. It wasn't right either way, and I knew that. I shouldn't have gone to her house after we had dinner at The Bistro. I should have driven home, texted my girlfriend, and gone to bed—that way when I got the phone call, I wouldn't have been in bed with another woman. Glancing at my phone, I wondered for a brief second if Corinne would think about calling me, until I replayed the scene of running out of her house leaving her in bed and half naked without saying more than five words to her in the process. God, it made me sick to think about how I must have made her feel. I would never want to hurt her. I'd loved Corinne since I met her, whether we were together or not.

While I was thinking about all that, Nicole's mom and sister came into the room. I tucked my phone into my pocket and quickly stood up. It didn't take long to fill them in on what the doctor had told me. Nicole was in and out of sleep, and everyone was getting settled in the room with extra things for the baby, like a personalized blanket and fuzzy blue socks. We all sat around quietly checking e-mails and our social networks while she rested. It was quiet. Too quiet for me. Since it was going to be a while, I offered to walk down to the cafeteria and get coffee for everyone.

In the cafeteria, I stood in line holding three small Styrofoam cups with flimsy plastic lids, and again my thoughts drifted to Corinne. I couldn't shake the guilt I felt toward her. Just knowing that there was no way at this point to make it right with her was killing me. I paid $9.75 for the three coffees, which seemed a little pricey, and began my walk back toward the elevators. I looked down at my watch; it was four a.m. I wondered if Corinne had gone to bed or not.

When I got back to the room, everyone was standing. Nicole was wide awake, and the doctor was checking her cervix. My heart dropped; I hadn't expected things to move along so quickly. I sat the coffees down and rushed to the doctor's side, feeling nervous—after all, this was my first kid. I kept asking him what was going on, but he just kept telling me to keep calm for Nicole. He said her cervix had jumped to an eight pretty fast and that he would be back in thirty minutes to check again. I didn't understand why we were waiting, but he reminded me that she needed to be at ten to push, then he left the room.

Nicole asked her mother and sister if they would wait in the hall and give us some privacy before she delivered. So they left the room, and, for the first time since I had been in bed with another woman, I was alone with my girlfriend. I reached out to hold her hand and felt mine tremble, so I pulled back, but she didn't seem to notice. She looked tired but still had a glimpse of excitement in her eyes. As we waited, we joked about what to name him, seeing as how we still hadn't chosen a name. I wanted her to feel calm and at ease, even if I didn't. What had happened with Corinne was without a doubt the worst thing I had ever done to someone. And to keep it from Nicole was wrong and unfair. But, in my defense, this was not the ideal time to tell my pregnant girlfriend that I was still in love with someone from my past.

I really did love Nicole, and I was going to be there for her and the baby no matter what. But what I had with Corinne was the kind of love that never fades, the kind that grows stronger through the good and the bad. I wasn't sure when, but I knew a conversation with Nicole would eventually have to take place; for now, I just wanted to make sure that she and our baby were healthy and safe. That was the most important thing. Before I knew it, the doctor was back to check on her. Sure enough, she was at ten, and it was time to push.

With her legs up in stirrups, I stood by her side and held out my hand for her to bear down on. She squeezed so hard that there was no way she could feel how shaky I was. She pushed with everything she had in her for a little over half an hour; I kept praying for him to come out soon. She was covered in sweat and starting to get weak, but the doctor urged her to reach deep within her and give it everything she had left. Inhaling deeply, she breathed out through her mouth and pushed hard for the count of ten, fingers twisted around mine, shaking, as the last bit of energy was forced out of her body, and then just like that he was here. The loudest cry came from his tiny mouth, and the doctor pulled him out and into clear view for the first time. My heart felt like it might explode when I saw his thick dark hair and his long, chubby legs. The nurses took him from the doctor and started suctioning his nose and mouth and wiping him down. I never once took my eyes off him.

When they brought our son back over to us, I let go of Nicole's hand so she could hold him in her arms. I watched her cuddling him, tears running down her face. Feeling overwhelmed by the most intense joy I'd ever felt in my life, I leaned over and kissed Nicole's head and began to cry. She looked up at me, tears falling harder now. She smiled and asked me if I wanted to hold my son. I couldn't think of anything else in the world I would rather do. I leaned over to gently take him from her so she wouldn't have to move or lift her arms much. As he lay nestled in the crook of my arm, swaddled in a thin blanket, I thanked God for such an incredible blessing. I didn't know what in the world I'd done to deserve something so wonderful and so perfect, but instead of questioning God, I just kept thanking him over and over with tears filling my eyes.

Nicole leaned her head back to rest but kept her eyes on us and smiled. She looked exhausted, but, my God, she looked amazing. I didn't feel like I could ever give back to her what she'd just done for me. But then I realized exactly how I *could* give her something. I would do the right thing and stay with her and raise our child together. She was a wonderful person, and I knew she was going to be an amazing mother. Besides, I wanted that for our son. I wanted him to have a mom and dad to come home to every day and eat supper and go to the park with. I wanted all that for him and so much more.

Nothing else was on my mind. No one else was on my mind. I held my son close to my chest and sat down on the bed next to Nicole. This was my family now, and this was all that mattered. Protecting them, taking care of them, and growing old together was what mattered. I kissed her again and thanked her for being so brave and strong. She smiled and told me she knew what she wanted to name him. I told her I would be cool with whatever she wanted. That's when she said, "Let's call him James." I'd never been more in love in all of my life. My whole world changed the moment my son was born. I didn't plan for any of it, but that's how life goes. And I did love Nicole. I've heard that comparison is the thief of happiness, and I think I finally got what that meant. I knew it wouldn't be the last time I thought about Corinne, but it would be the last time I made a decision that compromised our family. I couldn't let them down. As far as Corinne went, all I could do was pray that she'd forgive me. I looked at Nicole and then at my baby boy nestled against my chest, and all I could think was "This is love."

CHAPTER 21

SILVER LINING

Six weeks had passed since the birth of James' son, and Corinne hadn't heard from him once. He was wrong if he thought she wouldn't understand the complexity of his situation: the girl-friend, the baby, and being a father. She couldn't relate to these things personally, but she did understand what they meant. He had a choice to make, and he'd made it. It certainly didn't make her pain any easier to bear, but deep down she knew he was trying to do the right thing.

After spending a long weekend at her parents' house, she came home feeling rejuvenated and filled with a new sense of purpose, and stayed busy on her laptop for the next couple of days. After the original draft was complete, she spent a solid five days editing and rewriting. By the time she was finished she had a sixty-page short story. It was fiction, but she would be lying if she said the characters didn't hold a special place in her heart. When she first started the project, she wasn't sure what the purpose of it all was—it just seemed to be a good outlet for her, a place where she could release her emotions. But by the time she was finished, she had created a great love story. It wasn't "great" because of the fairy-tale factor or because of a happy ending; it was great because it was real.

She thought about James every day. She wondered how he was, if his baby had in fact been born a few weeks prior, and, if so, how fatherhood looked on him. She imagined it suited him well. Sometimes she caught herself daydreaming over the family they would never have, wondering if their kids would have her green eyes and his dark hair. Corinne knew she had every right to be furious with him, but she also respected him for the decision he'd made. Even though she believed he really did love her, she knew a significant part of him had loved this other woman too, at least enough to stay with her, and, in the end, that was what really counted. No one might ever have the same chemistry that she and James had, and she was finally okay with that—she had to be.

The holiday season was in full swing. Corinne's hometown was already decked out in blinking lights up and down Main Street, and there were wreaths on every light and telephone pole, and it was only Thanksgiving. She spent the long holiday weekend with her family, visiting grandparents, shopping with her sister, and just having some overall quality time with her parents. Her mom was actually doing really well and officially in remission, meaning her cancer was finally at a standstill. Her hair had completely fallen out, and she wore a different-colored head scarf every day, but she was slowly regaining her appetite and some weight. It had been a long time since Corinne had seen her mother happily singing and cooking in the kitchen, and that's exactly what she spent two solid days doing.

In other news, Ava and Andrew announced they were expecting a baby in early June, and the whole family was thrilled. It was the kind of news that gave everyone hope, that made a family feel alive with pure joy and hope. Corinne couldn't have been happier for her sister, and she knew she would make the best mom; this kid definitely wouldn't get away with anything. She wasn't sure if she herself would ever be a mom; she hoped one day she would, but for now, she was thrilled to be an aunt. Her little sister wasn't showing yet, but she was glowing just like they always say pregnant women do, and Andrew's eyes were alive with pride and excitement. Having a baby with the person you love was an exciting and wonderful thing. The weekend went by way too quickly, and before she knew it, it was time to head back to the coast.

Corinne and Charlie left early on Sunday morning. While her dad was loading her bags into her car, she talked casually with her mom about Christmas and blew on her coffee to cool it down. She hugged her mom tightly and walked out the front door with Charlie on her heels. The car was already running so it would be warm for her. She grabbed her dad in a tight hug, and they stood this way for a few minutes while her breath rolled like fog in the wintry air. For some reason she couldn't bring herself to let go. Leaving didn't used to be this hard for her. When they finally stepped back from one another, Corinne slid into her car and carefully placed her mildly hot coffee in the cup holder and shut the door, waving good-bye to her dad and feeling like a little girl again. His hands were deep in his sweatpants pockets and his face looked kind of sad, but he smiled at her and mouthed "be safe" just before he turned to head inside. Corinne sniffled. Charlie leaned over, putting his cool, wet nose against her cheek.

When they arrived home late that night, she let Charlie out to wander the yard while she unloaded the car. She unlocked the front door single-handed with somewhat of a struggle as she lugged her bags inside. Dropping them in the foyer, she went straight for her laptop and opened her e-mail.

When she'd finished her short story in October, she had e-mailed the completed draft to a small publishing company located in Brooklyn, New York. That was almost exactly four weeks ago. She had been checking her e-mail daily ever since. And today, there it was.

The e-mail read:

Corinne,
On behalf of Brooklyn Creations' literary editors, we are pleased to inform you that we have chosen your submission of "Girl Versus Fate" to be published. Our editors agree that your short story shows great talent, and we would be pleased to work with you.

We congratulate you again on your new partnership with us here at Brooklyn Creations and look forward to working on your narrative. If you should ever find yourself in the city, look us up. We would love to take you to dinner!

You can expect a follow-up e-mail from one of our editors within the next few days.
Best regards,
Samantha Harrison, Chief Editor

Corinne placed her hand over her mouth and gasped for air; she had been holding her breath without even realizing it. She started to cry, only this time it was with a huge smile spread across her face.

It had been a long time since she had taken responsibility for her own happiness, and when she finally had, it had welcomed her with open arms. She had always dreamed of visiting New York, and she decided right then that she'd use this as an excuse to go. She'd book a flight the next day and take them up on their dinner offer. Once in bed, she stared at the ceiling and imagined being in the city, covered from head to toe in cozy layers, wandering the streets and exploring the boroughs. Her eyes had started to feel heavy as her whole body relaxed and settled into the dense down comforter when she had the sudden urge to chug a glass of water. Reluctantly, she slid out of bed and dragged her feet slowly across the floor to the kitchen. The foyer lamp lit the small kitchen area just enough to find a coffee mug in the cupboard. Red mug in hand, she turned on the faucet and, when she looked up, sitting just a few feet away on the countertop was a small bouquet of red tulips wrapped in green tissue paper, a red ribbon tying them together.

Her mouth dropped open as ice-cold water overflowed out of her mug and ran down her wrist. How had she missed this earlier? Her head began to spin. Had James let himself inside and brought her tulips? Did he really still have a key to her house after all this time? This possibility surprised and excited her, but, more than that, it angered her. As if the first time around wasn't embarrassing enough, he had to leave another memento behind. This, at least, was easier to deal with than his naked body tangled in her sheets. She turned off the faucet, sat the mug next to the sink, and dried her hands on a towel that hung on a drawer knob. Examining the tulips, she admired their rich color and flawless shape. She held them close to her lips and breathed them in; they were perfect. Tucked underneath the red ribbon was a small white card folded in half. She pulled a loose strand of the ribbon and fumbled with the card nervously. There was a huge part of her that wanted to know what he had to say, although she couldn't imagine any combination of words that might change their history. She hoped for an apology or an explanation, but she knew a card of that size could only contain so many words.

She shut her eyes, still holding the card, rubbing its sharp edges and feeling the crease down the center. How could something so small cause her to feel so weak? Why did anything related to him hold so much power over her? Holding the card against her lips, she closed her eyes and foolishly wished there were such a thing as a time machine. But she felt pretty certain that her wishes had probably been used up at this point, and she could only picture him all snuggled up with his new family on this cold and dark night. It was a tough image to swallow, but, luckily, she had something else on her mind tonight, and that was the one wish that was actually in the midst of coming true. She took the white card, still folded, and placed it back down on the counter next to the beautiful reminder of what she wanted so badly to forget. *It will still be there tomorrow,* she thought, and with the comfort of that fact she went to bed.

CHAPTER 22

GOING, GOING, GONE GIRL

CORINNE

It was an early Monday morning and the Piedmont Triad International Airport was strangely quiet, but in a good way. The sky was still a deep-purplish-pink hue as dawn was taking place right before me. There's just something about catching a plane at dawn. Instead of waiting for the sun, you rise with it. There were only three other travelers waiting near the same gate as me, reading newspapers and checking e-mails on their phones and tablets. It felt like no one else in this town had anywhere to be besides home. Christmas was less than two weeks away, so I guess it made sense that most people would save the traveling till then.

From where I sat, two airplanes were in view, and I stared at mine anxiously. I started to feel a little antsy and had to stand to calm my nerves. I felt better reminding myself that it was a short flight to LaGuardia, and I was only going to be there for five days. My parents were more than supportive of the trip and immediately had offered to puppy-sit Charlie for me while I was away. So yesterday Charlie and I made our usual drive back to Winston-Salem.

When my alarm went off this morning in my old room at my parents' house, I was already laying there wide awake, just waiting for the signal to actually get out of the bed. I turned on a dim lamp that sat on the nightstand next to me and stared at the small white card, still folded in half, still a mystery. How I had been able to ignore it for this long was beyond me. Well, I wouldn't say I'd been ignoring it, exactly, maybe more like procrastinating. Who knows, perhaps I wouldn't read it at all. I mean, that was always an option, right? I had not factored in time for a mental game of tug-of-war this morning, so I left the card on the bedside table and started to get ready.

I stepped into a pair of dark-blue skinny jeans and smoothed my hands over my thighs while examining myself in the vanity mirror, then I chose a neatly pressed floral button-up from a hanger that dangled on the closet door. I buttoned it up to the collar and pulled on a thin royal-blue sweater over it. A fun pair of patent leather black wedges would complete my outfit. I looked trendy, but, equally important, I looked intelligent. My parents' room was just a few feet away, so I carefully tiptoed down the hallway, into the bathroom, and closed the door. I brushed my teeth and splashed cold water on my face multiple times until I felt alert. I went through my usual makeup routine, which took no time at all. The apples of my cheeks sparkled, and my lashes were ultra dark. Lastly, I applied a clear gloss to my lips and leaned over the sink to examine myself closely in the mirror. I tossed the tube of gloss in the trash can and pulled out a bold lip stain called "Cherry Tulips." I'm not sure if that was a coincidence or fate or maybe my subconscious obsession with all things tulips. Whatever it was, I applied the lip stain, twice. Finally, to tame my wild, wavy mane, I spritzed my hair with a coconut-scented texturizer.

I turned the light off and snuck back to my room, where I grabbed a floor-length wool coat; *I would definitely be needing this in New York!* I pulled my purse over my head, wearing it across my body, and stuffed a few loose items into my suitcase before zipping it up. Charlie was still snuggled in the bed; he never once got up while I was getting ready, like he wasn't worried because he knew I'd be back for him. I leaned over to kiss his wet nose, just to be reminded of what I didn't have, or more accurately, *whom* I didn't have. I was torturing myself, really. I could end all this turmoil by tossing that little white card straight into the trash. That idea sounded great, even kind of cool, but who was I kidding, I wasn't going to do that. Even though I couldn't leave it behind, I was still avoiding the inevitable, so I put the card in my back pocket. By the time I got downstairs, my parents were already up and waiting on me at the kitchen table. I should've known they wouldn't have missed my send-off.

"Honey, you look amazing!" my mom said immediately.

"I can't tell ya how proud we are of you," my dad added.

I smiled, feeling eternally grateful for these two people, who had brought me into the world and given me the skills to conquer anything; and for the times I couldn't, they instilled in me the confidence to fearlessly press on. I hate that I lost it for a little while, but I guess losing yourself is a part of life, and it's actually okay to do, just as long as when you get it all figured out you come back more fierce than ever.

"Don't make me cry; this stuff isn't waterproof," I said, grinning and pretending to dab at my eyes.

They helped me out to my cab, which had arrived five minutes earlier than expected. The driver was standing outside smoking a cigarette but was careful not to litter when he saw us walking down the driveway. He promptly put out the cigarette on the road and wrapped the butt in a tissue he spit into and stuffed it in his pocket; kind of gross, I know. He looked a little rough with his ponytail hanging out from under his trucker hat, but I wasn't judging. He loaded my bags into his cab while I said my good-byes. I hugged them both before ducking into the backseat of a very nontraditional cab. It was a brown van with large white sticker letters going down the windows that read "Big Vick's Cab Service." I was excited at the thought of hailing a classic yellow cab in the city.

Standing side by side and holding hands, my parents waved in the direction of the van as we pulled off. I turned to wave back and watched them until they were out of sight. The drive was quiet; Big Vick didn't have much to say, but I was appreciative of the silence and enjoyed some downtime with my thoughts. It was roughly a thirty-minute drive to the airport, which I used to check a few e-mails and download some new songs. When we arrived, it was still dark outside, and Big Vick pulled his van up to the drop-off lane. He came back around to my door and opened it for me, even offering a hand. I smiled and accepted his gesture, returning the favor by giving him a generous tip. He nodded his head, stuffing the small wad of cash into his back jean pocket, and pulled off. With an hour to kill, I got through security with ease and was on a direct mission to find coffee.

Now the sun was almost completely visible in the sky, and I could feel the heat permeating the windows and warming up my whole body. My coffee had cooled down a little, so I was taking more frequent sips and feeling much more relaxed. My coat was folded and neatly laid on top of my bag just a few feet away. The closer the time came to board the plane, the more lone travelers started appearing, making their way closer to the gate. I couldn't believe that in just a few short hours I was going to be in New York! This was the exact kind of journey I had always dreamed of, ever since I'd started writing, but at some point I guess I forgot how much it meant to me. It was sad really to think about how quickly a dream could become just an idea you once had.

Thoughts of the past suddenly redirected my attention to James. I'd be lying if I said I hadn't thought about him every day since our last face-to-face encounter. The truth was he was on my mind a lot, and I was sure that even years down the road, a piece of him would always remain with me. But at least I was moving forward, and that was a promise to myself that I knew I could keep. I had put the pain and emotions that followed the night we almost spent together into my writing. In doing this, I was able to sort of remove myself from the equation and write a *fictional* narrative based on true events. It gave my heart and head a voice, while giving me some much-needed perspective.

Writing it all down might be the closest that James and I would ever come to having closure, and that was totally fine with me. I'd realized that closure wasn't all it was cracked up to be. Sometimes there are not enough words, opportunities don't always present themselves, and, to be blunt, there is no possibility of closure.

I watched out of the windows as luggage was being tossed like rag dolls underneath the plane and quickly checked the time on my phone. I tipped my paper coffee cup straight up and downed the last sip, holding that position for a few seconds, wishing there was a little more left in the bottom, when a lady's voice crackled over the speaker announcing that Flight 147 to New York was now starting to board. I threw my coat over my arm, my bag over one shoulder, my purse crisscrossed over the other shoulder, and headed toward the gate. After waiting in a short line to board, I pulled my ticket out from my back pocket and let the attendant scan the bar code.

As I walked through the gate, I could hear the roaring engine and feel the vibrations under my feet. Each step I took, I became more electrified with excitement. Maybe it was the coffee, or maybe it was because this was the best day of my life, but I couldn't stop shaking. I crossed over the hatch and smiled as I made eye contact with the pilot. He was a distinguished older man with salt-and-pepper hair, very attractive. He winked at me as he sipped his coffee from a small Styrofoam cup, and I felt myself blush. I easily found my spot—a window seat, thankfully—and stuffed my bag into the overhead compartment before getting comfortable. I tucked my coat and my purse under the seat in front of me and looked out across the sparkling tarmac. It was then that I decided to finally read the small white card that was folded in half and delivered to my home with a bouquet of red tulips just weeks before. How I waited this long without so much as peeking at it was beyond me.

Reaching into my back right pocket, I retrieved the note from James. I guess being on a plane felt safe, like I was at a safe distance and nothing or no one could reach me. I unfolded the card, and the first thing I noticed was it was handwritten with a black ink pen. There were no smudges, no eraser marks, just small, legible scribble, half print and half cursive like he always wrote. With each word I could hear his voice and see his face; my heart raced and a lump formed in the back of my throat.

Corinne,

Please forgive me for not being able to be your everything, but know that you are and always will be everything to me. I'll always love you.

Forever,
James

The sun beamed brightly through the plane windows, causing me to squint, but really it was tears that blurred my vision. I bit my lower lip and pulled the note against my chest to steady my shaking hands. He was releasing me. After all these years, I could finally let go. I looked out the window and noticed a blur of color lining the asphalt in the distance on the other side of the landing strip. Spotty images of pink, red, white, and yellow dotted the far-off landscape, and the foggy double-paned plane windows made it difficult to see clearly.

The engines picked up, and I could feel the power of the machine stirring underneath my feet as I leaned closer and pressed my forehead against the window. The plane started to move forward and line itself up to prepare for takeoff. The humming grew louder as we rolled slowly at first but quickly picked up speed, and just as the plane lifted into the air I was able to clearly see the brilliantly colored field from a different angle. I finally realized the plethora of bright colors staining the field were rows and rows of blossoming tulips; flying higher in the sky now, I could see more colors than I first thought: purple, fuchsia, and orange scattered among reds, yellows, and pinks. It was like a tulip factory, mass producing flawless flower after flower on an assembly line. It was an extraordinary farewell, the send-off of a lifetime as I said good-bye to a part of my past that I could no longer carry with me. Only the memories would remain, but that was okay; memories were fine to hold on to just as long as they weren't holding on to me.

The higher the plane flew, the more the colors began to mix and dissipate and soon vanish altogether. I finally understood that some love just wasn't meant to last. There wasn't a good guy or a bad guy, and there certainly wasn't a winner or a loser, just two people going in different directions with two separate lives to lead, and that was all right. It wasn't a great love story because of some happy ending; it was great because it was real. Thousands of feet in the air, I could see clearly for miles, and I admired the beautiful landscapes of North Carolina as I whispered, "Good-bye."

EPILOGUE

CORINNE

Well, this was it. The beginning of a new chapter in my life, and I had a clean slate to write it however I wanted. No time to dwell on love and the past; my new mantra was all about me: rediscovering myself as a writer and a single woman. Oh, who was I kidding? I was a sucker for a good romance and all that came with it, good or bad, but after the way my last relationship ended, I was pretty sure it would be a while before I ever fell in love again. It was no one's fault, really, but the saying is true—timing really is everything, or at least a solid 75 percent.

My flight was a short one, so there was no need to take a catnap, not that I could've fallen asleep anyway. I happily accepted the complimentary coffee served on the plane and daydreamed about my future as a writer while the creamer swirled in the Styrofoam cup. As we flew into the city, the only thing illuminating the grand skyline was the sun itself. Judging by the thick clouds rolling in, it didn't look like the sunshine would last for long. From the sky, buildings looked like thousands of tiny Legos stacked vertically and then strategically placed next to one another to fit as many in a designated area as possible.

The pilot announced over the intercom the near-freezing temperature outside, not unlike most winter days in New York. The sun came out just long enough to consider it a sunrise and then disappeared behind a cluster of billowing white clouds. The plane landed in the middle of a light winter rain that bordered on the verge of actually being snow. Just outside the gate, I set my bags down and put my coat on. Convinced it wouldn't be enough, I kneeled next to my suitcase and began to dig. It didn't take me long to find my thick-knit red infinity scarf and faux black leather gloves. I loaded myself down with my bags, keeping my purse conveniently draped on one shoulder and hanging across my chest.

I made my way quickly through the crowded terminal, reminded of why I was so glad I hadn't checked any luggage. I scooted sideways through the crowd, keeping my hands close to my side for safety like when on a roller coaster. Edging my way into an empty space on the escalator, I leaned in to catch a ride to the lower level. I caught my balance by instinctively grabbing hold of the nearest object, which happened to be the sleeve of a tall, skinny man's coat. I smiled at him, feeling a little embarrassed, and mouthed the words "I'm sorry." He didn't respond. I definitely felt like a true tourist already, and I was smiling way too much, at everyone. Where I'm from we say hello to strangers and let people with just a few items go ahead of us in the checkout line. We also instinctively smile at people for no reason at all.

Outside, the rain had already turned into snow, and taxi cabs were taking off with travelers just as quickly as they were arriving. I stood still for a moment like a deer in headlights watching the madness: hand gestures that I didn't even know the meanings of, streaks of yellow as taxis were dodging other cars, and the constant buzz of cell phones, iPads, and the monotonous chatter that tied it all together. A blizzard-like gust of wind whirled through, causing my eyes to squint and my body to tense up. The snow blowing at such a rapid speed was stinging my face, and I was now focused on the mission at hand, getting a taxi for myself. I took a few steps forward toward the pickup/drop-off lane where a few empty cabs had just pulled up. Clearing my throat in preparation to use my outside voice, I started with "Excuse me, sir, I . . ." That was all I managed to get out when a short, stumpy women with crazy brown curls pushed past my left shoulder shouting about some place I've never heard of and threw her hand up clenching a wad of cash. *That's it,* I thought, *money will surely get their attention.* The stumpy lady waddled faster than any waddle I have ever seen, and the taxi was peeling off before I could find my wallet blindly with one hand.

Frustrated with the disorganization of my purse, I reached in deeper, with both hands this time, feeling around for anything with a zipper. *Ah-ha!* Completely in my own world as this point, I was fondling my wallet and didn't see the seven-foot-tall man come barreling toward me wearing a warm-up suit and wool hat. Apparently he didn't see me either, because he stomped on my foot, and it felt like he crushed every single tiny bone. All 250 pounds of him landed heavily on my right foot, and my knees buckled. Letting some choice words fly in my head, I would've screamed them had I been able to breathe at the moment. He glanced back at me quickly while I was all but on the snow-and-salt-dusted concrete and threw his hand up apologetically. I noticed some thin white strings hanging out from under his hat and realized he was wearing earbuds right as he shouted "Sorry, ma'am" way too loudly. My teeth were clenched and so was my fist around my wallet. *At least he was polite.*

Okay, it was time to get serious. I had been standing outside for nearly ten minutes, and it was getting cold, like really cold. The feeling in my face was starting to go away, all except the painful burning frostbite sensation in my nose and cheek area. These cheap gloves were more for looks than they were for actual warmth, and my fingers could barely grip the zipper as I finally started to open my wallet. My frozen pointer finger stiffly sorted through the cash, and I found a few twenties surrounded by a bunch of ones and a fifty-dollar bill. Just as I began to pull out a twenty, another blustering wind came howling through and ripped the twenty, along with my only fifty-dollar bill, from my grasp. The two bills danced around each other in circles until the twenty got swept away by the momentum of a passing taxi. The fifty fell to the ground less than ten feet away as the wind died down. Not bothering to zip up the wallet, I dumped it in my purse and started toward the cash. Just before I reached it, two thin, well-dressed women crossed my path, trampling my money and sending it flying again. It hadn't gotten too far, so I picked up the pace and broke out into a careful and inconspicuous jog down the snowy sidewalk. My money was teasing me just a few feet away, unable to come to a complete halt, and seemed to be rolling faster and tumbling farther with each step I took. My subtle jog turned into a creepy, hobbit-like run where my back was hunched over, my knees were bent, and both arms were stretched out in front of me, fingers stretched straight. The wind started up again, and the money swirled and spun along the sidewalk, getting heavy and limp from the snowfall. I was gaining on it, and I could see Ulysses's face as clear as day, when suddenly, I lost my footing. My patent leather wedges were without a doubt adorable, but the soles were as slick as the ground was quickly turning. I started to slide, and then overcompensated by trying to slow my run back to a jog and lost my balance. Inertia and gravity took over. I bowed my back, my arms flailed, and just before I crashed to the ground where I would surely fracture my tailbone, I closed my eyes to prepare for the fall. But it never came.

I peeled my eyes open slowly to examine my situation. Much to my surprise, I was not lying on the icy ground. That's when I noticed him. His grip was strong as he steadied me in his arms. My back rested on his chest, my legs were sprawled out in front of me, and the lower half of my torso hovered just inches above the snow. The pant leg of a well-tailored suit and a black leather wingtip shoe was visible between my thighs. Embarrassed, I attempted a graceful recovery and tried to pull my legs together but slipped again on the ice as soon as my feet made contact with the ground. I felt his weight shift underneath me as he started to fall with me but caught himself by balancing on one hand, knuckle deep in the snow. I could tell he was pretty agile from his quick and careful movements. I realized I owed this stranger, big time. Even though my fifty-dollar bill had vanished by this point, along with my dignity, at least I wasn't all banged up. Besides, this wasn't the most embarrassing thing that had ever happened to me, so I knew my ego could handle a beating way better than my fragile bottom half could.

He maneuvered his feet to stand up straight and used his forearms like a forklift, wrapping his arms underneath mine and bringing me upright. Still facing away from him, I regained my stability and held my position like an ice sculpture until I was certain I wouldn't fall again. His hands had moved to my waist and were still holding tightly, like he could tell I was reckless. As I turned to face him, his hands stayed loosely in place, sliding across my back and grazing my sides. But before any words could come out, my mouth dropped slightly at the sight of his bright-blue two-toned eyes and sandy-blond hair, clean-cut and short along the sides and styled longer on top; his lips were full and in clear view due to his freshly shaven face. He wore a dark-gray suit, tailored to fit his exact build, a skinny black tie, and a crisp, pressed white collared shirt underneath. I needed to say something to him, and quickly, before he noticed how deeply I was inhaling his cologne.

"Thanks" was all I managed to get out.

"Anytime." He smiled, simultaneously winking.

"I was trying to . . . I was chasing this . . ." I continued to stammer. "Basically, someone ran into me and, well—"

"Is this yours?" he interrupted, holding a fifty in his left hand.

"Seriously? How did you even . . ." I considered speaking in full sentences, I really did. I reached for the bill, but he pulled it back just out of reach.

"You want to grab a drink?"

"Umm, it's nine a.m."

"Coffee?"

"I've had plenty this morning."

"Dinner tonight, then."

It sounded more like a statement than a question, and I rolled my eyes, feeling slightly annoyed but admittedly enjoying his attention and efforts more than anything.

"Well . . ." I paused. "I actually have a business-type dinner meeting thing tonight." And that was the honest truth; however, I wished I had sounded more confident in my reply.

He smiled and looked extremely sure of himself for a guy who had just gotten shot down three times. I'm not going to lie, it was kind of sexy. Just before handing me the fifty-dollar bill, he leaned over and said, "You're not from around here, are you?"

I stood up straighter, trying to pretend I had no idea what he was referring to. "Why do you say that?" I asked.

Instead of an actual response, he just looked me up and down. Twice. I pretended not to be affected by him but was secretly swooning over the attention way too much. He handed me the money but not before making some pretty heavy eye contact with me and saying, "Have a good stay. New York will love you."

I pulled the bill carefully from his grasp, sliding it upward from his fingers while he held my gaze, our eyes staying focused on one another.

"Don't you mean, *I* will love New York?"

With the raise of an eyebrow, he adjusted his tie and said, "Yes, that too," and walked away.

For a brief moment, I watched him like the last remaining doughnut in an otherwise empty box, but the feel of a warm, dry fifty-dollar bill caught my attention. It was way too crisp and new to be mine. After all, mine had tumbled in the snow for some time. There was no way this was my money! "He must have . . ." My words trailed off at that realization, and when I looked around, he was nowhere in sight. The New Yorker in him had already hailed a cab and was on his way to wherever he was going. I couldn't believe it. He was like my guardian angel, only insanely hot and wearing a three-thousand-dollar suit. Welcome to New York.

ACKNOWLEDGMENTS

To my husband for always looking out for my best interests and for his unwavering support while I follow my dreams. To my extraordinary daughter, who inspires me every day to be a better person and to make choices for a brighter tomorrow—in case you ever forget, you are everything.

To my parents for encouraging my passionate nature and for convincing me at a very young age that I could do anything I put my mind to. To my incredible sisters, who have always had my back no matter what—with you two by my side I am truly fearless.

To my "bonus families" for all of your positive and constructive feedback while I worked on this book and for always treating me like your own daughter. To my truest friends for being insanely supportive and proactive in helping this dream of mine come true.

To everyone at Inkshares and Girl Friday Productions for this amazing experience and for guiding me through this publishing journey.

Also, I would like to thank my dogs for their loyal companionship since the day I rescued them.

ABOUT THE AUTHOR

Photo © 2015 C. McNamara

Kacie Davis Idol lives in Kernersville, North Carolina, with her husband, beautiful baby daughter, and beloved dogs. *The Tulip Factory* is her debut novel.

LIST OF PATRONS

This book was made possible in part by the following grand patrons who preordered the book on Inkshares.com. Thank you.

Adam Gomolin	Emilie Siler
Anna Hugli Knowles	Erika Lane Clark
Barry Davis	January Marie Flynt
Brenton Purcell	Jennifer Evans
Cameron Ligon	Jeremy Thomas
Catelin M. McNamara	Jeri Crowder
Chelsey Ann Bryan	Jim Bryan
Cher'e Sorrell	Jimmy Idol
Cheri Lingafelt	John Taylor
Chris Idol	Joseph Fox
Chris James	Joseph M. Weavil
Connie Crowder	June Forshee
Dr. Daniel J. Bryan	Kerri Bumgardner
Debbie Lee	Krista Crowder Davis
Deborah R. Loggins	Lauren A. Robertson
Donna Idol	Manda E. Stack
Ellen W. Comer	Dr. Mark R. Cowan

Megan Hulen
Michael Shawn Crowder
Nicole Bruno Cox
Page Trimble
Pam Barrans
Patrick McNamara
Robert Duggan
Scott Cole
Shea Smith
Stephanie Charles
Teresa Cook

Thaddeus Woodman
The Idol Family
The Street Boutique
Time Remembered Quilting
Timothy Taylor
Tina Andrews
Wes Atkins
Zach Pruitt
Zach Sheets
Zack D. Zando

INKSHARES

Inkshares is a crowdfunded book publisher. We democratize publishing by having readers select the books we publish—we edit, design, print, distribute, and market any book that meets a preorder threshold.

Interested in making a book idea come to life? Visit Inkshares.com to find new book projects or to start your own.